22ND A. ... ... INTERNATIONAL

3-DAY NOVEL-WRITING CONTEST

SKIN

a novel

BONNIE BOWMAN

ANVIL PRESS

VANCOUVER • BC

Skin

Printed and bound in Canada
Cover design: Dean Allen, Cardigan.com
Author photo: Lincoln Clarkes

CANADIAN CATALOGUING IN PUBLICATION DATA

Bowman, Bonnie 1955–
Skin

ISBN 1-895636-32-9

I. Title
PS8553.O907S54 2000   C813'.6   C00-910042-3
PR9199.3.B636S54 2000

Represented in Canada by the Literary Press Group
Distributed by General Distribution Services

The publisher gratefully acknowledges the financial assistance
of the B.C. Arts Council, the Canada Council for the Arts, and
the Book Publishing Industry Development Program (BPIDP)
for their support of our publishing program.

Anvil Press
Suite 204-A 175 East Broadway,
Vancouver, B.C. V5T 1W2   CANADA

To
Did

With thanks to my long-suffering parents, Doris and George, for their lifelong support and forbearance. Their suspicion I was switched at birth will undoubtedly be strengthened by reading this.

And special thanks to Brian Kaufman who was there to slap my bastard child on the ass and give it life, after a painful three-day birthing process.

BOOK ONE
The Freak Show

DR. NATHAN SWAN struggles with his perverse desires, stemming from what he perceives as his hideous deformity. CYNTHIA POOLE worships her own skin, paying little attention to what lurks underneath it. BOTH ARE CONSUMED WITH THEIR APPEARANCE, UNAWARE THE GROTESQUE IS ABOUT TO SUPERIMPOSE ITSELF ON FRIVOLOUS BEAUTY.

I

O ver the ice cubes and onto his tongue. A burning finger of whiskey slid down his throat and
into his belly. Soon it would make its way up and
into his head. That's what he was really waiting for.
He poured another one, his hand shaking with
anticipation as he raised it to his lips. It was the
third time this week, the spells were becoming more
frequent. He didn't think he could ignore this one
though, didn't think the whiskey could stop it, numb
it. A pain behind his eyes, in his groin. His free hand
clenched and unclenched as a sheen of sweat washed
over his forehead despite the cool conditioned air.
The air! He stumbled over to the balcony door,
breathing shallowly, fumbling with the lock. The
heavy glass pane glided back and he lurched outside, gulping. But it was no better. He had forgotten
his sunglasses, the ocean glinted crazily and it was
hot, too hot. He stuck out his tongue, felt like he
could lick the air. The sun was too bright and

7

squeals from the beach slammed into him. Squeals of tires, of laughter, music. Usually when he felt a spell coming on, he found the ocean view from his Kitsilano condo calming. But today, it was an assault. That's when he knew he couldn't stop it.

He walked back into the living room. A light touch, and the door rolled shut behind him. He poured another shot, added more ice, and paced silently, thinking.

There was only one thing he could do to relieve this pressure. The thought made him nauseous, but there you have it. Walking over to the leather reclining chair, he laid back into it and unzipped his pants, not looking. He knew what he'd see, the cause and the cure for his sickness. Staring at the ceiling, he pulled his silk boxer shorts down with one hand, took another drink with the other. Freed, his penis lurched out of his pants. Or more accurately, the creature uncoiled like a grotesque balloon animal, untwisting in slow motion. His freakishly large member waved slowly back and forth, seeking. Allowing his gaze to slip downward, he looked at it with disgust. It was completely undignified. *An obscene prick.* All his life, it had only brought him grief.

It started with his father and a bathroom door that didn't lock properly. The first time a much younger Nathan saw his father taking a piss. He had pushed the door open and stood there unobserved while his father's hot urine steamed into the toilet. Nathan was impressed with the velocity and curious about his father's penis. He had never seen his parents, or anyone else, naked before. His father finished his business with a perfunctory shake, and turned. The pair stared at each other for a beat. Then his father spoke.

"Don't you knock?"

He hurriedly zipped up his pants and busied himself at the sink.

Something was amiss, but Nathan was oblivious. He took a step towards his father.

"Dad? How come your *thing* is so little?"

His father took a long time drying his hands on a towel, staring down at the boy. At the time, Nathan couldn't articulate the look he was receiving from his father. But whatever happened in the bathroom that day was just the beginning. His father treated him differently from then on.

"Maybe you should ask your mother that question," he said, pushing Nathan out of the way as he left the bathroom.

Nathan never did ask his mother, he just figured things shrunk when you got older.

But after that, his father got weird. Nathan thought it was his fault somehow, and kept his private parts private. *Don't ask, don't tell.* To make paternal relations worse, Nathan was a sickly youngster with weak lungs and bad eyesight. At age four, he had been fitted with ugly blue-framed glasses. None of this impressed his father, who wanted a strapping son to play ball and hockey with. Nathan gave it his best shot, tossing endless balls to his father on the lawn.

"You throw like a girl."

Skating, falling over on his weak ankles after five minutes of hockey.

"Get off your ass, Mary."

It didn't take long before his father gave up. They were drying their hair one day after Nathan had made so many grievous blunders he thought his father was going to belt him one. But his father simply looked defeated. That's when he started making comments Nathan didn't understand.

"Guess it doesn't really matter. Don't think you'll have any problem impressing the girls, once they get to *know* you."

Nathan had no idea what he was talking about. After the feeble attempts at athletic endeavours were history, his father started drinking more. He would have his buddies over to watch football and Nathan could sometimes hear his father talking about him in a loud voice. He would make references to Nathan's stick handling, going deep, getting good wood on it, slam dunk thank you ma'am. The neighbourhood men would roar and spill their beers and punch Nathan's father on the arm. Nathan didn't get it. He sucked at sports.

And school. The showers, the first time his boyhood classmates had seen his penis. The first time he had seen any other boy's penis. Nathan had eluded the showers for a long time, owing to respiratory problems that prohibited him from participating in Phys. Ed. classes. But eventually, the sadistic instructors found ways to get him involved as a gofer. Ways that landed his butt in the showers with the rest of the teams. It had been humiliating enough just taking his clothes off in front of those boys. Boys who were used to stripping in company. They who swore and spit and could always outrun him. Damian Hasselbach had been the first to notice. You could hear his hooting from the shower room all the way down the hall.

"Holy shit, man! Take a look at Science Boy!"

He had been startled then, standing with his with skinny, mole-speckled back to the other boys in a corner of the shower. He didn't think anyone could see him. But as the shrieks slid off the slimy walls and the wet, naked boys started to gather around, he turned to look at them, confused. For an instant, as he stood there with his glasses still on, wet and fogged up, he had a crazy thought. *They're talking to me! Are they being friendly, finally?* He managed a shy smile, and wiped the fog off his glasses to see. But they weren't being friendly after all. They were doubled over laughing and pointing at him and although he was accustomed to being tormented, this was different. Their jeers had an unfamiliar ring, one he had not heard before. It didn't occur to him until years later that it might have been awe, or envy. But by then, it was too late. It took a second, but he finally realized what they were pointing at. He was horrified. Automatically, he looked down at himself, thinking something was wrong. But aside from the fact that he was completely exposed, a position he found unnerving in the extreme, everything seemed in order. Until he dared to look at the other boys, dared to look between their legs.

"Hey! Freakenstein!" Hasselbach crowed. "Whatcha do? Grow that in your LAB?"

He was mortified. A freak. His eyes burned, and he tried to run from the shower, slipping on the soapy tiles, his big dick slapping his thin wet thighs, as he stumbled into the naked boys who were grabbing their own penises and swinging them around like little propellers.

"Hey look out, don't trip on Science Boy's shlong!"

"What do you *want?*"

Snot now, blurred vision, strange hands grabbing wildly at his penis, pulling on it, head bowed, small delicate hands trying to cover his disgrace, impossible, a nightmare.

"How big's it get when you get a boner?"

"You could put out an eye with that thing!"

He had finally made it out of the shower that day, but he never really left.

He tipped another shot into his glass. It was time. Leaning over, he fumbled around in the drawer beside the chair. His left hand found a magazine, his right hand crept towards his crotch. It was a *Playboy*, an older issue, but never mind. It was either going to work or it wasn't. He prayed this time that it would. He opened the magazine at random, Hello Miss January. Not good enough, he wasn't partial to redheads. He flipped a couple of pages trying to find a brown-haired woman. His freak of a penis was painfully swollen, had been for a long time now. He found her. Charity Heatherton. Not likely, he thought grimly. *I like pizza and lifeguards and I want to be a dental hygienist.* He smirked. *Oh yeah, well I like whiskey and peelers.* She was beautiful, in all her airbrushed splendour. But his perversity demanded this trial of perfection. Charity pretty much stacked up with her long, brown hair and improbable breasts. Here was Charity in thigh-high boots and a Nazi cap, ass to the camera, bending over a chair with her fingers up her pretty little snatch. There was Charity in a pink lace garter belt reposed on a canopy bed, long white legs spread wide open, a peach of a pussy front and centre. Charity in buckskin, in leather, in glorious smooth ivory skin. His right hand began to move slowly, evenly. His eyes were glued to Charity's charms, maybe it would work this time. His right hand picked up the tempo. Please Charity, he begged silently. *Help me.* Faster now, faster. Come on, Charity, come on. Keep it smooth, don't think, concentrate. Charity's red lips smiling at him. *She likes me.* Come on, come on. Flagging a bit now. *No!* Charity's green eyes inviting him. We're losing it. *No!* Pain now, humiliation starting to creep in. *We're losin' her, captain.* Still his right hand valiantly keeps the rhythm. Charity's red lips sneering at him. Charity's green eyes mocking him. *The betrayal! The bitch! Fuck!* His right hand falls away, his left shoves Charity onto the floor and grabs his drink. A gasp, a gulp of Scotch. Two minutes he sits like this, then looks at his penis. As he expected, it's reviving. It moves a little, like a freckled frog taking a hop. Then it lurches spasmodically, and laboriously unfurls itself again. Erect, the freak is taunting him. He sighs, resigned. Gets up from his chair and walks into his study, his nemesis bobbing heavily in front of him, eager. It knows where it's going. He closes the venetian blinds and sits at his desk, pushes the papers to one side and selects a book from the shelf. It is a big book, a large hardcover medical text. He opens it slowly, regrettably almost, but knows which pages to look for. The pages with the women, of course. Some are naked and some are not, but these women don't have names. He finds one of his favourites. She is standing in only her skin looking right at him, but no fancy poses, no make-up or costume. She does have brown hair. He wondered what her likes and dislikes would be. *I like organic fruit and doctors and I want to be healthy.* His right hand seeks its place under the table. His left index finger traces the woman's body. Her skin is bright red and peeling off in large patches. New fresh skin is exposed in spots, excruciatingly vulnerable. His right hand begins its work and the freak responds, an obedient child now. He traces her poor diseased flesh with a practised finger and can almost feel the scaly roughness. His eyes close briefly and he's filled with compassion and urgency. He turns the page, another woman, close-up of her face. A grey tumour under one eye. A tear comes to his. Bites his lip and flips to an autopsy. A thick layer of yellowed fat clings to sawed-off ribs, a milky, lifeless cataract stare – she must have been about sixty – and he can almost smell the decay. Flips again, a malformed pendulous breast with two split nipples, each leaking viscous fluid. Another page, translucent albino. Hallelujah.

Dr. Nathan Swan masturbates violently, successfully. He shudders.

I I

CONCERNS THE APPEARANCE OF CYNTHIA POOLE, BOTH LITERALLY AND FIGURATIVELY.

Cynthia Poole was doing one of her favourite things. She was looking at herself. Not in a psychological way, you understand; not one of those inner searches. No, Cynthia Poole was getting down and busy in front of her mirror. If you take care of the outside, the inside will take care of itself. It's so simple. When you look good, you feel good. And Cynthia Poole looked good. Yes, superbly good indeed. But Cynthia Poole never took her looks for granted. Why, only yesterday she had turned twenty. No longer a teenager, but a young woman. And even though she had always taken care of herself, this was no time to get complacent. She examined her young woman face intently, elbowing aside her lotions and astringents and powders for a closer look. No wrinkles she could see yet. She smiled broadly at herself, checking her dimples, poking her fingernails into them. Still intact. She pulled her skin back tightly on her face and let it snap into place. Instant perfect face again.

Merciless blue eyes scrutinized every familiar detail. Her nose was slightly too prominent for her face but it gave her a somewhat regal quality. Thank you Princess Diana. Her hair was her glory. Blessed with thick straight hair, she had kept it long. Streaked it so it was almost entirely blonde. She was a master, or a mistress, at morphing her mane into any shape or style and she had an unerring instinct for when to wear it up and when to set it free. Today it was tied back in a simple high ponytail. Her face was glowing from a recently peeled melon masque. Bright, fresh and youthful. Pleased with her reflection, Cynthia Poole selected an exquisitely tiny jar of cream and removed the gold lid, staring at herself as she did so. A slender finger dipped into the cool silky cream, skimming off just enough to dab on her right cheekbone. Absorbed in her reflection, she dipped again and meticulously applied bits of the cream to selected areas of her revitalized face. Then delicately, sensuously, she blended the velvety coolness into her greedy skin. Humming quietly, intent on her task, she selected a different jar of cream for her neck and – eyes closed, head thrown back – generously swathed her long neck in age-defying decadence. Wiping her hands, she let the straps of her slip fall from her shoulders. A large bottle now. Great blobs of pale green aloe-based lotion smearing her shoulders and down her upper arms. The slip had fallen off further, a bit of lace getting hung up on her nipples. The goddess stood, silk slithering down to her tiny waist. She turned her music up, Diana Krall, recklessly squirting more lotion into her slippery palms. Across her upper chest now, her hands sliding in ever smaller circles, caressing her curves with knowing, practised fingers . . . smooth, greasy, circling inwards . . . inwards, hips swaying to the piano. Loving herself. Now an airy spin, silk falling to the floor. Kicking it aside with one painted toe, she grabbed the lotion bottle and sang into it, *Peel me a grape*, dancing lightly, slick breasts swinging. Extending her slightly rounded tummy as far as she could, she squeezed another glob of green cream onto it. Her blonde ponytail swung as she spun around the room, hands smoothing lotion on her hips and pelvis, fingers engaged in a daring dance. Her long legs were newly shaven and dry, so dry. Cynthia Poole went crazy on them. Long ribbons of cream down each slim white limb. She danced and sang and smeared, cream dripping onto her pearly toes, her silver toe ring, onto the burnished hardwood floor of her bedroom. She slipped while trying to execute a *cruzada*, but righted herself, squirting more lotion onto her magnificent ass. Bent over a chair, she luxuriously massaged the cream in, looking over her shoulder at herself in the mirror as she did so. She liked what she saw. All dewy and damp, pretty, she thought. *Pretty in pink*. Cynthia Poole's face was getting flushed now, her entire body tingling. She stood up straight and flung the ribbon from her ponytail, letting her hair fall past her shoulders. While she cupped a breast with one hand, she grabbed the bottle of lotion with the other. Shaking her heavy hair, she held the bottle out and turned.

"Will you do my back?" she asked, panting slightly.

"Sure, baby," he said.

III

↷ INTRODUCTION TO MARIANNE WEDGE, A
PERIPHERAL CHARACTER WHOSE PRESENCE SERVES
TO FURTHER ILLUSTRATE THE DAMAGE AND DOWN-
FALL CAUSED TO A YOUNG MAN WHO KNOWS TOO
LITTLE AND HAS FAR TOO MUCH.

The walls were wood panelled and a monstrous
hi-fi sat in the corner. Shag carpet, scratchy
records, posters, black lights. But it was the 1960s,
and rec rooms were teen terrain. Parent-free zones
and panty-free zones. The parents in this particular
case were Mr. and Mrs. Donald Wedge. They were
upstairs. Marianne, their beloved daughter, was a
bit of a mousy girl if truth be known, but feeling
especially frisky this night. She had just returned
from the golf course where she had consumed the
better part of a mickey of gin while huddled under a
footbridge at the ninth hole. Mr. and Mrs. Donald
Wedge were drinking rye and Coke in the kitchen
and playing a game of Scrabble. While they were
getting triple-word scores upstairs, Marianne
Wedge was taking off her flowered panties down-

stairs, aiming for a single score. The hopeful benefi-
ciary of Marianne's gracious deflowering was her
biology partner who had also attended the golf
course that evening. A quiet, serious boy by nature,
he was turning off the lights while Marianne fumbled with her clothes.

"Should I turn the music up?" he whispered,
knocking his knee against the stereo.

"No, leave it. They'll come down if it's too loud."

"Where are you?" he asked, feeling around desperately.

"Over here, on the couch."

Hands outstretched, he felt his way over to the
couch. Wooden coffee table, cool glass ashtray, gin
bottle, empty air, woollen cushion . . . soft, warm
flesh! He pulled his hand away like he had just
touched his mother.

"Sorry," he mumbled.

"What are you sorry about?" Marianne asked
teasingly, grabbing his hand with her own and
putting it back on her thigh.

"I, nothing," he said, closing his eyes as she
guided his hand across her smooth belly.

Soft, so soft! He had never felt anything like it,
her skin didn't even feel like skin. It felt more like
the hairless baby mice in biology class.

"Come here, closer," she said, grabbing his shirt
collar and pulling him down onto the couch.

Awkwardly, they settled in, lying on their sides
facing each other in the dark.

"Take off your glasses," Marianne said, fingers
pawing at his face.

"Okay."

Wire-framed glasses clattered onto the coffee

table and a tongue probed the general area of his mouth. He parted his lips, allowing her sloppy explorations.

"Aren't you going to take your clothes off?" she asked. "I've got my panties off. But don't take your pants all the way off in case my parents come down."

He nodded in the dark and half sat up, his face bearded with rank saliva. It was confusing. Part of him, a very specific part, was thrilled to be here but the rest of him wasn't so sure. His stomach felt like it inevitably did when he was on a swing. That swooping feeling, ecstatic nausea. He had never found Marianne particularly attractive, but he couldn't see her in the dark, which helped. He pictured her being Sondra Shoemaker, the class beauty, and he throbbed harder. But if he had to think about it, he wasn't really enjoying the kissing, Marianne's breath was foul, stale gin and cabbage. He struggled with his fly and pulled himself out of his jockeys.

"Have you got it out yet?" Marianne asked from her reclining position.

"Uh, ya," he said.

"Feel me up first," she demanded.

He lay back down trying not to press his hardness against her too much, and groped around for her tits. She was holding her blouse up over her face. His hand found one round small breast and he cupped it joyfully, his thumb rolling the nipple around. Marianne made a sound like a pigeon, so he lowered his face and put the adorable nub into his mouth. With one hand holding her breast to his mouth, he let his other hand wander south under her skirt. Marianne was starting to writhe around and he was beginning to doubt her proclaimed virginity.

That could be a problem, he thought. She'll know I don't have a clue.

"What time is it?" she asked.

His hand jerked away from its walk-about down under.

"What?"

She struggled up to rest on her elbows.

"What time is it?" she repeated, grabbing his left wrist and trying to see his watch.

"Um, it's about eleven," he guessed.

"Shit! I have a midnight curfew, we better hurry up if we're going to do this."

Marianne wriggled around and wormed herself onto the couch on her back, manhandling him on top of her. Dropping one leg onto the floor, she cranked the other up against the wall. He was in prime position now and ready to burst. He made a few futile stabs that only succeeded in bruising her inner thighs.

"Stick it in!" she hissed urgently.

Rattled, he grabbed his penis with his right hand and with his other hand, felt around the mystery lands for an opening. His fingers sank in a bit and he readied his penis for entry, hoping he was on target. A stanchion poised over the sinkhole.

"Is this . . . ?" he spluttered.

"Hurry!"

Armed with that specific lack of guidance, he held his breath and heroically plunged into Marianne Wedge's undefiled depths with all the pent-up frustration and unresolved guilt a young teenage boy could muster. Marianne let loose a lung-splitting scream, causing Mr. and Mrs. Donald Wedge to drop their vowels and bolt down the stairs.

Turning on the lights, they were greeted with a spectacle such as they could never have imagined and after that night, could never erase. Their dear little Marianne sprawled motionless on the couch, legs akimbo, blood seeping into the afghan her grandmother had knitted, and Nathan Swan's monstrous dick half stuck up inside their daughter.

While Marianne was rushed to the hospital to get stitches, and what would be the first in a lifelong series of therapy sessions, Nathan Swan was shipped off to the police station where he sat for hours under a horrible bright light, blinking wildly without his glasses, feeling shame and panic and Marianne's blood drying on his offending prick.

Years later, Mr. and Mrs. Donald Wedge would describe that incident to their bridge partners as they swilled back their booze and chainsmoked their Sportsman cigarettes. They laughed about it and rolled their eyes, but every time they related the story, Mrs. Donald Wedge got a curious yearning *down there.*

IV

☞ A PIVOTAL MOMENT IN CYNTHIA'S CHILDHOOD
IN WHICH SHE TAKES CENTRE STAGE AND
SUBSEQUENTLY FALLS OFF WITH A DISTINCT
LACK OF GRACE.

Cynthia Poole was six years old and her head hurt. More specifically, her scalp hurt. She was sucking on a cherry popsicle, wearing a scratchy bib, and sitting on a high stool in her mother's white kitchen. She could hear her friends playing outside on neighbouring lawns, and the child part of her that was still intact longed to rip the screamingly tight rollers off her head and run outside. But she had not been allowed to play outdoors for weeks now. She might get a bruise or a scratch or, *God forbid child*, an unholy tan. For the past month she had been coming straight home from school to practice piano for an hour. Then she would march around the living room for half an hour with a cookbook on her head. After that, she would stand in the bathroom on a chair and sing scales for an hour, watching herself in the mirror to make sure she didn't scrunch her face up too much when she hit the high notes. There were plenty of other things Cynthia Poole would have to do every evening too: read poetry she didn't understand, practise dance lessons, take scented bubble baths. There was no time to play with her friends, even though Cynthia Poole was a very popular child. Before she went to bed, her mother would brush her long brown hair a hundred strokes, and pat her down with powder that made her eyes itch. She would place a cool hand on her forehead as she lay in bed and kiss her cheek. Her mother always smelled like fruit, and Cynthia Poole adored her mother in the way that only fear will inspire.

"Where did you get that?" Gladys Poole shrieked now, grabbing the dripping popsicle from her daughter's hand and lobbing it into the sink.

"Lord, child, do you know how hard it is to get cherry stains off your mouth?"

Wide blue eyes blinked benignly, meeting accusing grey ones. Gladys Poole slumped slightly and began vigorously wiping down the red lips, muttering under her breath, her large bosom pressing into Cynthia.

"I wore a bib, mummy," Cynthia said faintly.

"Yes, that's very nice dear, but we don't want you to have red lips today. Today, we want you to have pink lips. Don't you remember that lovely frosted pink flamingo lipstick I bought for you? You can only have red lips when you wear that darling little number with the feather boa and fishnet stockings. Remember? Remember? God!"

Gladys Poole scrubbed the pouty lips with a vengeance. Cynthia thought it best not to mention how much her head hurt. She knew this afternoon's audition was very important to her mother. It was big, the biggest. The one that would get her a movie deal and make her a star. She remembered hearing her parents talk about it when they thought she was getting her beauty sleep.

"This will be it, Bert," Gladys had said. "This is the one. Our little Cyndi will be famous one day and this is the one to do it."

Bert Poole had simply grunted and sucked on his pipe.

"It fuckin' better be. Because if it ain't, I'm shutting this business of yours down. It's costing me a fortune, all these pageants and shows and crap. You know we need a new truck, but all your shopping and trips and bloody photo shoots are keeping us in the poorhouse."

Gladys nodded, knowing she always got her way. Besides, she knew Bert was secretly proud of their little Cyndi. She'd seen the way he looked at her when she was all made up and wearing her prettiest party dress. He'd bounce her on his lap and smell her hair. And when she got down from his embrace, Gladys had seen the look in Bert's eyes. He always looked sort of sad. So Gladys knew that despite her husband's protestations to the contrary, he liked seeing his baby being the prettiest one on the block. The *block*. Hell, the *world*.

"Listen honey," Gladys said, putting a hand on his leg and leaning into his shoulder.

"If Cyndi gets this part tomorrow, you can buy a hundred trucks. Why do you think I'm doing this? I'm doing it for us baby, so we can have a better life."

Bert puffed and squinted.

"Well, alls I'm sayin' is she better do good tomorrow 'cause if she don't, I'm pulling the plug on this whole damn business."

"She'll do good, honey," Gladys said. "She'll do good, I know it."

Cynthia withdrew from her place at the top of the stairs and silently tiptoed back to bed. Her bedroom was filled with snapshots of her life, poster size. Cynthia as a baby in a christening gown, Cynthia with a wide toothless smile in a Jell-O ad, at a pageant wearing a tiny sequined gown, holding roses and being crowned, Cynthia at the beach in a yellow bathing suit holding up a bottle of the leading sunblock. There were no pictures of Cynthia eating birthday cake with icing all over her fingers and face, laughing in a mud puddle, or hanging from a tree with twigs in her hair and scratches on her knees.

She climbed into her canopy bed and lay there, staring at the white lace sky, seeing faces and animals in the patterns. She better do good tomorrow. Daddy needs a truck.

The next day flew by and after her lips had been scoured of the demon popsicle, Cynthia Poole's long hair was released from its tight torment. Gladys lovingly combed out the ringlets with slender, practised fingers and sprayed, primped, twisted and scented until not one hair dared defy her. Into the powder room with its large mirror ringed with light bulbs and under the expert steady hand of Gladys Poole, Cyndi's fresh scrubbed face transformed into flawless porcelain with frosty pink lips, rouged cheeks and strategically placed individual long brown eyelashes fluttering under immaculately

tweezed and brushed baby brows. Drop pearl ear-
rings quickly inserted into soft tiny ear lobes, shiny
pink nail polish expertly applied to dainty finger-
nails and toenails, a green taffeta dress with black
lace and black crinolines, iridescent stockings and
shiny black shoes with bows and princess heels.
Finally satisfied, Gladys pushed her daughter out of
the powder room.

"Go show daddy how you look," she urged.

Cynthia walked down the stairs like she was
taught, one hand lightly on the bannister, smoothly
on the balls of her feet and turned slightly to one
side. Slowly, daintily, head held high, not looking
down.

Bert Poole looked up from his newspaper when
she was about halfway down and watched her
descend with ease. She reached the bottom and
walked slowly towards him, with a bright smile and
looking just above his head at the wall. When she
was two feet in front of her father, she did a perfect
twirl that caused her dress to spin out prettily and
then she curtsied.

"Well, daddy . . . ?"

Bert Poole stared hard at his daughter and then up
at his wife a few steps behind her. Both were looking
at him for approval. Gladys, with her tired face and
sloppy belly. Cyndi with her shining hair and painted
lips. Bert felt uneasy and knew he couldn't even
touch his daughter right before an audition or
pageant. She might get mussed up. She might break.
The familiar pain in his stomach flared.

"You look good Cyndi, real pretty," he managed.

"Thank you daddy," she giggled, doing an
impromptu twirl that almost showed her panties.

"That's enough now Cynthia," said her mother, descending the last couple of steps. "Save your moves for the director."

With that, mother hurried daughter out of the house, leaving father behind to drink a large glass of Maalox mixed with brandy which he immediately vomits into the sink.

"Places please! Quiet on the set!"

A young girl had just finished her audition for the upcoming feature film, and was now crying hysterically in her mother's lap. She was getting mascara and make-up all over her mother's nice lavender dress and her mother just absently patted the girl's head. They both knew they were finished. They had driven for two days to get here, but now it was all over and everyone knew it.

Gladys Poole cast a sympathetic glance at the stage mom, and took a few more tranquilizers. She'd lost count. Cynthia was standing quietly beside her, observing things and being a perfect angel. Cynthia knew everything was riding on this audition, everything. All those other pageants, the lessons, the torture, it all came down to this. For the first time, she was nervous but knew better than to tell her mother. She also knew better than to tell her mother she had twisted her ankle the other day at school playing on the monkey bars. And Cynthia knew absolutely for *Christ Jesus* sure not to tell her mother she had taken one of her nerve calming pills. Or was it two? She didn't remember. Her head was kind of fuzzy. In fact, she had felt like laughing when that other girl had made such a mess of her audition.

You stink, she thought, suppressing a giggle.

"How are you doing, honey?" Gladys whispered, leaning over.

"Fine mummy. I can't wait." she said, too brightly.

Gladys narrowed her eyes, searching her daughter's face, but finding only God-given perfection aided by her own masterful handiwork, she relaxed and smiled.

"You're next baby, make me and daddy proud."

Cynthia Poole smiled at her mummy and skipped to her mark. The lights were so hot, Cynthia felt like her hairspray was melting and the set was so quiet it made her jumpy. A nice man was holding her lines for her on a big card, but the words were kind of moving. An adult actor was off to the side waiting for his cue, a handsome young actor – she thought she might even recognize him – who was her pretend daddy.

Cynthia lowered her voice so it would tremble slightly, like she had practised, and, widening her eyes, she said her first line.

"Daddy? Daddy, where are you?"

She looked around the set, ringlets flying.

"I can't see you daddy! Where did everybody go?"

Gladys Poole was on the edge of her seat, heart beating out of her chest, lips moving, mouthing the lines.

A male voice curls out from stage left, the handsome young actor.

"I'm here sweetie, you just can't see me. Walk towards my voice."

Cynthia spies the young actor, thinking, what an idiot, I can see you. She takes a few steps and then remembers she has a line, but forgets what it is. She stops, shakes her head, and swivels around looking for that guy with the card. But he isn't there anymore. He's moved with her, he's in front of her now, holding the card. She looks forward again and spies him. Oh! She grins and then remembers she's supposed to be scared.

"I'm coming daddy! Don't leave me here alone!"

She walks slowly, head cocked for the voice, looking around.

"That's it, honey, not much further," the male voice coaches.

But the voice seems to be coming from another direction. Confused, Cynthia stops and looks back. The card man rushes over and she stares hard at the words but can't seem to read them. Her heart starts picking up speed and she looks frantically for the actor.

"Daddy?" she says in a tiny voice, ignoring the cue card guy.

"Over here, baby," she hears from another direction.

Turning too quickly on her princess heels, her ankle twists and pain slices up her leg. Cynthia trips and falls into a table on the set, grabbing her ankle. Gladys is half out of her chair, hissing, "Get up, get up you little fool."

Righting herself, Cynthia turns in a circle, looking for the voice, and getting scared for real. The lights are too bright and too hot, the words on the cards now like tiny worms, and she starts to hiccup uncontrollably. Frozen, she stands in the middle of the stage, arms outstretched, turning in circles, hopping on one foot, and all she can remember to say is *Daddy, where are you?*

The director throws down his cap, and gets off his chair. The young male actor comes out from his position, and Gladys is stumbling towards the stage clasping her chest. Cynthia continues twirling and hiccuping, twirling and hiccuping, and singing. The other mothers are staring at the scene with a strange sense of sympathy mixed with absolute glee. The girls are awestruck and pleased with the performance, some are clapping. Cynthia starts giggling at all the commotion and feels sick to her tummy. The director is leaning over her, saying nice warm things and the young actor is crouched down in front of her saying things like, "It's all right." She looks at the actor and says, "Hey, you're not really my daddy," and finds it all quite amusing until she looks up and sees her mother coming towards her.

Gladys Poole towers above her daughter, swaying slightly, and she's got a very red face and a funny look in her eyes. Cynthia starts to panic. Gladys says something to her but it comes out weird, like she's speaking another language, and her mouth twists up in a scary way. Her mother's hand reaches out to her daughter, but it looks like a claw and Cynthia shrinks back from it, starting to cry. Gladys croaks something out that sounds like a monster and Cynthia pees her pants. Right on the stage. People are running around now, barking orders, and men are laying her mother down on the floor. Cynthia just stares, forgotten, standing in her pee, and sucking her thumb. She knows she did something bad but she just can't think of what that is right now. Her mother is reaching for her with her claw hand, but Cynthia cowers back. She covers her ears and closes her eyes and hums. When she feels a warm hand on her shoulder and opens her eyes, her mother is all covered up in a sheet, even her face, and being carried away.

Someone leans down in front of her and says, "Where's your daddy, honey?"

Cynthia Poole looks up at the nice lady and opens her mouth to speak, but nothing comes out.

"Your daddy, honey? Where is he? We should take you home."

Cynthia Poole looks at her mother's body disappearing around a corner. She opens her mouth again and screams. She doesn't stop screaming for a very long time.

V

☞ NATHAN FINDS HIMSELF IN VANCOUVER'S
DOWNTOWN EASTSIDE SEEKING ANOTHER
OUTLET TO RELIEVE HIS DESPAIR.

Dr. Nathan Swan is cruising the downtown east-side of Vancouver in a rented car. This part of town, bordering the ocean, is the city's ugliest boast. Most crime per capita in Canada, or some such statistic he recalls reading in the paper. Down here, heroin competes with crack cocaine for the users and the used. *Uptown, downtown.* Every storefront, every alley, every block, one of society's discards claims the sidewalk. Some have needles hanging from their scarred arms, some are beaten and bloody, some already dead. Most of Nathan Swan's colleagues have tried to patch up the aftermath of the downtown eastside's effects on its denizens. None, he would be willing to bet, have ever ventured down here. It's too ugly for their refined country club tastes. Tonight it is raining and the sidewalks and streets are slick with detritus awash in shimmering neon. The junkies are huddled under awnings, the prostitutes stand shivering either from the cold rain or their own inner painful heat. And the cops are either chatting amiably to a familiar hollow face or putting an aggressive chokehold with thick black leather gloves on someone with strength enough to fight. Nathan Swan drives slowly, peering at the sidewalks through the slapping of the wipers. He is not one to judge. The scene down here neither disgusts nor delights him. But it does suit his purposes. No one who knows him as *Doctor* Nathan Swan would ever find him here. Here he can be anonymous, which is how he feels most of the time anyway, and his peculiar aversion to beauty isn't compromised on these streets. He is accepted down here, without question. No one asks what he does for a living, no one cares what he looks like. They only care that he has money. And that's one thing Nathan Swan does have. His earlier session with the skin book hadn't been enough to dull the need. This was an insistent craving, and he was jonesing for a fix. He had long ago given up having sex with so-called *real* women who either laughed nervously when they saw his large cock or were afraid of it, or gushed on and on about its magnificence but then couldn't even get their pursed collagen-injected lips over the head of it, let alone their uptight society cunts. And word got around. He couldn't go anywhere familiar without feeling the eyes of the local women on his crotch. Or the eyes of their husbands, narrowed and suspicious. He had lived in Toronto then, when he was going to med school and subsequently starting his practice in dermatology. But once word got out about the freak in the medical community, he went underground. Avoiding contact with anyone other than his patients, turning down dates, not knowing which type of rejection from women was worse, that from strangers or from women who had been forewarned and took him on as a challenge or a dare. Didn't matter, they all treated him like a novelty act at first, like shit later. *Run away, little girl.* Then he ran away, with his dick between his legs.

In high school, it was the sluts. After word somehow got out about Marianne Wedge, the sluts actually started looking at him. Like a fool, he took their notice as a compliment. He, of course, didn't know they were sluts. To Nathan, they were the popular girls. Not in his league, no siree, but after the *incident*, Science Boy started getting some attention. Susan Babcock, with the biggest tits in school and a mass of red curly hair, must have drawn the short straw. She was the first to approach him. Got him back to her place on a lunch hour – seemed all the sluts had working parents who were never home at lunch – and got the first look-see at what all the fuss was about. Good old self-assured, big-titted Babs, was probably on a dare, but Nathan figured she would redeem him. Marianne had probably freaked out about nothing, he thought, as he watched Babs pull her tight T-shirt up over her head. He had stared in amazement as her massive breasts dropped free from the shirt, bouncing, heavy, obscenely large pale nipples. *Great! They're huge.* He remembered thinking maybe she was a freak too. At least she probably wouldn't faint when he whipped the bad boy out. And Babs, being one of the popular girls, wouldn't be a virgin. That could have been the problem with Marianne, he thought. Susan Babcock had stood there then, with all her crazy red hair flying around her face and her gi-normous boobs, hands on hips, staring at him. He did nothing, didn't know what to do. But Babs did. She knelt down between his legs as he sat in the E-Z Boy recliner and unzipped his fly. Nathan laid back into the chair, eyes closed, feeling her hands struggling to pull him out. She knew what she was doing. Everything was going to be all right. He would be vindicated. Babs would suck him, or fuck him, and she'd go crazy for his big cock, and run back to school and tell all the other popular girls, and everyone would have new respect for him, and all the guys would envy him, even the teachers, and maybe, just maybe, he could lose the shame, the feeling that he was somehow bad, no good.

But that just didn't happen. Once Babs finally dug the big guy out, Nathan had felt nothing. Her fingers on his dick, yes, but silence, nothing. No movement. He had opened an eye then and looked down at her, dreading what he would see. It was a look that would become all-too-common. A look that, every time Nathan saw it, would make him feel sick. Susan Babcock had her hands full, but she also had a reputation to uphold. She was holding his cock with both hands, staring at it, with the kind of look you get when you first get handed mescal and you know you have to drink it, worm and all, to be cool. So you squint your eyes, hold your nose, and down it, squealing with disgust, shuddering and spazzing out for about thirty seconds after. Babs was in a quandary. She had to report back. So, to her credit, she squinted her eyes, held her breath, and opened her mouth. *Okay, that's more like it.* Nathan held his breath too, wondering if a popular girl

could actually take him. Poor Babs's mouth was
stretched so tight, her eyes were watering, and from
his position, Nathan thought she looked horrific,
like she was wearing some kind of mask. She barely
got her lips around the head of it, and then with a
grunt, forced about an inch of it into her mouth that
was dripping saliva from the corners. She started
making a weird *hunh-hunh* sound and it looked like
her eyes were rolling back in her head, saliva now
flowing freely onto her chin. Nathan watched fascinated, worried. Then Babs looked like she was
turning blue. It was like she was stuck there, her
fingers scrabbling at his shaft, bile rising in her
throat, her huge breasts shaking, stomach heaving,
until finally with a supreme effort, her fingers dug
painfully into Nathan's dick and she snapped her
head back with a sound like one of those airlock
doors. Nathan slumped further into the chair, hands
covering his penis. He didn't know what to do. He
could tell he was red in the face. After she finished
gasping and spazzing out, Susan Babcock wiped the
back of her hand across her mouth and stood up. She
grabbed her T-shirt and struggled back into it. She
looked at Nathan and pointed to the door.

"*You* are fucked," she said, panting.

Nathan leaped out of the E-Z Boy recliner and
was out the door before Susan could say another
word. As he ran home, embarrassed, trying not to
cry, he felt truly defeated. If the prettiest girl in
school thought he was a freak, he didn't stand a
chance. If anyone would know, she would. He was
right. The next day at school, the popular girls who
had once only ignored him, now mocked him. He
didn't get angry. He transferred. The anger came

years later, after the night he stood in the kitchen with a knife to his dick but couldn't bring himself to use it, and before the night he resigned himself to the freak's existence.

After having transferred once again, to Vancouver this time, Nathan made sure no one ever saw him naked. Monks and nuns lived without sex, or so everyone was supposed to believe. But Nathan, try as he might, couldn't be that saintly. He could dampen his drive with drugs for a time but he had a libido as preternatural as his penis and once his system adjusted to the *drug de jour*, he would fall prey to another attack from within his own ranks. Sometimes he could alleviate his compulsion with masturbation. But other times, like tonight, that just wasn't enough. So now he cruised the inner city streets, one hand on the wheel, the other pressuring his crotch, rubbing it. He had bypassed the hookers further south, the girls with the designer clothes and make-up, slender shapely legs and pillowy cleavage. After his earlier attempt with that bitch Charity, he was forced to acknowledge that pretty girls still made him feel sick and angry. He was better off down here with all the other fringe freaks. Their scabbed faces, skinny bruised legs, and dirty clothing. Pathetic, he needed pathetic and there was plenty to choose from. Sometimes the glorious array of imperfect flesh was overwhelming. It was so hard to decide. Turning down a side street, he spotted her. A bit separate from the other girls, a calf cut from the herd. The rental car glided smoothly to the side of the road and sat there idling. The young hooker spotted him and sauntered over to the passenger door. With a flick of a button, the window rolled down about six inches and she stuck her nose in the car, sniffing him out. They stared at each other for a minute and a glimmer of what could pass as recognition flickered in her pinned eyes.

"Get in," he said, unlocking the door.

The girl, who couldn't have been more than seventeen years old, folded her skinny self into the front seat and turned to look at him.

"I know you," she said. "You were down here last month with Amber."

Nathan nodded, lit a cigarette and offered her one. She took it.

"Could have been," he said.

Feeling a little more at ease, the girl gave him a good once over.

"You're the dude with the big cock, aren't-cha?"

Nathan nodded, exhaling a cloud of smoke.

"That's me."

"Well, whaddya know? Amber said you were a pretty decent guy," the girl said, her grin exposing rotten teeth. She extended a scrawny hand.

"I'm Tawny, pleased to do ya."

Nathan shook her limp hand and could swear he heard tiny bones crack.

Pleasantries exchanged, Tawny spoke next.

"So what'll it be Big Boy? Blowjob, half 'n half, straight lay? Don't worry, I bet I can take all of ya."

Nathan unzipped his pants and let his seat fall back a few inches. He closed his eyes, feeling the beast rear up and bump the steering wheel.

"Just a blowjob."

Tawny butted her cigarette, moved her face closer.

"Holy fuck, man!" she said, when she saw it. "Amber wasn't shittin'."

But quickly recovering, she went into her rap, leaning in, her lank hair falling into his lap.

"Hey, you big, bad boy, you're so-o-o-o hard, I'm gonna cum just lookin' at ya."

Nathan looked down at the top of her head and noticed patches of bald scalp and flaky dried skin. He almost went off right then and there.

"Don't talk," he said. "Just suck."

"Aye aye," said Tawny under her breath, deftly manoeuvring a condom into her mouth before she made her final descent.

Although Tawny had obviously mastered the trick to opening her throat, she still couldn't do justice to Big Boy. But she was good with what she could handle and Nathan appreciated and needed it. He looked down at her while her head was pumping the freak and noticed each bony knob of her cervical spine. He pictured her without clothes on, a skinny beat-up wretch no better than he. Then he mentally undressed her further, taking all her poor sad skin off, envisioning a skeleton giving him a blowjob. That did it. He exploded into her mouth, shooting the condom halfway down her tired throat.

VI

CYNTHIA DOES WHAT SHE DOES BEST . . .

Cynthia Poole handed the bottle of lotion to Derek, who lay sprawled on her bed, naked, glorious. He took his hand off his handsome prick to grab it, and smirked up at her.

"Fabulous," he drawled. "Lie down next to me."

Cynthia, slippery and sweetly scented, walked to the bed and undulated, belly first, onto the black satin sheets. She lay there, humming quietly to the jazz music filtering into the room, her pretty bottom swaying. Derek squirted the lotion into his palm and began massaging it into her upper back in slow, sensual motions. She giggled when he trickled cool, tiny droplets down her spine and into the crack of her ass. She shivered when he ran his finger down the same path, and her long white legs parted slightly. Derek squeezed lotion into both palms and grabbed her ass firmly, massaging his way to her inner thighs. Cynthia moved her legs further apart. Derek, never one to miss a cue, knelt between her legs. And while he stroked his superior cock with one slick hand, he

41

teased her with the other, thinking *choreography is everything*. Cynthia's perfect posterior raised up slightly and Derek grabbed her firmly now, pulling her up in one quick motion. He held his breath and slowly, evenly, pushed himself halfway in, holding a beat, almost out, slowly back in a ways, and . . .

"CUT!"

Cynthia and Derek froze and both looked over to their right, annoyed.

"Sorry folks, I mean, hold it a sec, I have to reload," said a skinny, long-haired guy hanging over the bed, fumbling with a camera.

"Rigby!" Cynthia sulked, twisting around and pushing Derek off her.

"What's with this 'Cut!' crap? You're not Steven-fucking-Spielberg, you're just shooting my promo shots. I don't have all fucking day, y'know."

Rigby, frantically reloading, thick glasses falling off his nose, shrugged, embarrassed.

"I'm sorry Cyn, I guess I just got caught up in the action, sorry."

Cynthia pouted and rolled over onto her back. Derek sat on the edge of the bed, a startlingly hand-some young model. He still had his cock gripped firmly in hand, stroking it with adoring pulls. Cynthia glanced at him and rolled her eyes to the ceiling. She sat up on one elbow and lit a cigarette. The lotion was sticky now and she felt like she needed a bath.

"Hey, Rigby, maybe you got enough, huh? You got me dancing, stripping, and at least one shot of Derek's brilliant dick sliding into me, didn't you?"

Rigby snapped the camera back into working order and looked up with his crazy, buggy eyes pin-wheeling behind his glasses.

"You don't want anything else, then? No cum shots?"

Derek stopped stroking and looked over at Cynthia, bored. He could care less, he would get paid anyway and besides, women didn't really turn him on.

Cynthia sat up and shrugged, grabbing her sarong and deftly wrapping it around her.

"Look Rigby, just give me what you've got later today, and I'll take a look. If I think I need more, we'll set it up for another time, okay?"

Rigby licked his lips nervously.

"Okay, Cyn, I think we got some good shots here."

He clumsily picked up his camera gear and shambled out of the room.

"I'll call you in a couple of hours," he said.

Derek got dressed and looked at Cynthia.

"That dude's probably going to go home and take a cold shower."

Cynthia looked up at him with distaste.

"Who, Rigby? I doubt it. He's a professional."

Derek arranged his profitable penis comfortably in his pants, gave it a loving tap, and saluted her.

"See you around," he said, and turned on his heel.

Cynthia watched him go, relieved. She walked back over to her mirror and stared at herself. Grabbing a towel, she started removing the grease from her skin. She had a movie shoot tomorrow, she should get some sleep. Hopefully it would be one of the last movies she had to do for Cecil French. They paid the bills, and quite well thank you very much, but with Rigby's pictures and her audition tapes and extensive work with French, maybe she could land a gig with Jerome's outfit. In porn circles, that would be the big time. Better pay, better working conditions, better lighting, and a make-up and wardrobe staff. Shit, she would even have dialogue that made sense. Hell, any dialogue would be a challenge. Yes, Cynthia had a plan. And although it was a little known fact, she knew some of Hollywood's top actresses used to work for Jerome. If Jerome would accept her into his stable, the sky was the limit. And Cynthia Poole was so hungry, she felt she could eat the entire sky, stars and all.

VII

"Dr. Swan. Your ten o'clock is here."

"Thank you Marjorie," Nathan said into the intercom. "Give me a couple seconds."

Nathan flipped through the chart on his desk. Bobby Brightman. Chronic *acne vulgaris*. Or in layman's terms, very, very bad acne that will never get you laid. Poor kid, he thought, recalling the lad from a few weeks ago. Guess the tetracycline wasn't doing the trick. The loser had tried those damn bioré strips before he had seen him last. Those nopest strips that cute, perky teenage girls on television used. *Look ma, no flies on me!* At the time, Nathan had tried not to laugh out loud. *What were you thinking, boy? A girly bioré strip? Fuck, you'd need two rolls of industrial duct tape slapped onto those bleeding pustular lesions and ripped off with pliers to even touch that mess.*

But he had gently told young Bobby that bioré

45

strips were only for light blackheads. And although Bobby had so many, it looked like blackflies were breeding on the swamp he called his face, the kid had worse problems to deal with. Red, oozing lumps for starters. He sighed, writing out the next prescription he would try, knowing already what he would see when Bobby walked in. His young face festering, his young soul crushed with humiliation. Even when his acne cleared up in adulthood, he would be left with scars on his face that only cosmetic surgery could heal. But Nathan knew surgery would do nothing for the other scars that Bobby would always carry with him. You can't burn those off or dig those out. You can only cover them up. Make-up for the soul. Some people called it therapy. Nathan called it bitterness.

But he would be glad to see Bobby, nonetheless. He enjoyed patients who were truly suffering. What was insufferable to himself, were the young beautiful girls who came in with a nasty rash, or a mild case of eczema marring their baby-smooth skin.

"But Doctor Swan, it looks like a hickey! My boyfriend will kill me!"

Not if I do first.

"But Doctor Swan, it's right here on my chest, how can I wear my low-cut dress to the prom?"

Maybe you should have thought twice about getting those unbelievably fake tits before you bought a push-up bra and shoved them in everyone's face.

"But Doctor Swan, isn't there some kind of special make-up I can use to cover it up?"

Years of therapy, you tart.

"Dr. Swan? Are you ready for Mr. Brightman now?"

Nathan stood up to greet Bobby, and adjusted his concerned yet kindly smile on his face.

"Yes, Marjorie, send him in please."

Bobby Brightman opened the door to Nathan's office and turned to look at him. It didn't take a professional to tell that Bobby was worse. Nathan strode over and casually flung an arm around the boy's thin shoulders, leading him to the chair.

"How are you feeling today, Bobby?" he asked in his best doctor voice.

Bobby Brightman opened his mouth and then just collapsed, quiet sobbing, his head hanging down. Nathan gave him a couple of seconds, and Bobby lifted his head again, trying vainly to control his outburst. His eyes were leaking, his nose was leaking and, worst of all, his entire face was leaking.

"Duh, Doctor Swan," he gulped noisily, his voice hitching.

"Yes, Bobby," said Nathan, reaching for a clean wipe.

"I can't take this any, any more," Bobby stuttered. "I really feel like sometimes I could kill, kill myself, Doctor Swan."

Nathan's heart took a dive, and he quickly came around his desk to comfort Bobby who was shaking and weeping on everything.

"Now, Bobby," Nathan said, giving him a firm hug. "You might not believe this, but sometimes I want to kill myself too."

Bobby's sniffling slowed down a bit and he turned his pitiful face up to Nathan's, eyes wide.

"You do?" he asked.

Nathan nodded sagely and walked to his intercom.

"Marjorie, please tell my next patient I'm running behind. I'm going to be awhile."

He looked over at Bobby and gave him a genuinely warm smile. He picked up a mirror, and a photograph of Bryan Adams, and walked back to the boy.

"Okay, Bobby, let's talk."

VIII

☞ HOW A PHONE CALL LIFTS CYNTHIA'S SPIRITS
AND GIVES HER RENEWED HOPE FOR THE FUTURE.

Cynthia Poole was sitting by her phone. Rigby's photos had been superb, and she had done a couple of decent flicks with Cecil in the past month. Contacts had been made, and she had met last week for lunch with a rep from Jerome's. It was all going to happen for her, she could feel it. Lunch had gone well, she thought. She had worn her tightest whitest dress, and re-streaked her hair. High-heeled white pumps enhanced her long creamy bare legs and she didn't wear any stockings for the interview. Hell, she'd even flashed the creep some Sharon Stone action when he bent over to pick up a napkin. The mousy rep had looked appropriately flustered and she caught a glimpse of him in the bar mirror admiring her posterior through the filmy material as she wriggled her way to the bathroom.

Now she tapped her manicured nails nervously on the phone, willing it to ring with the good news. Three o'clock. They said they'd call at three o'clock to give her an audition time. She smoked a cigarette, inhaling deeply, and stared at herself in the mirror above the phone table. Impulsively, she leaned over and kissed her reflection, leaving a peachy imprint on the glass. She licked it. *Come on, come on.* Ten past three. She butted her cigarette, hand shaking. She wet her finger and squeaked the lip marks off her mirror. Stood up and stretched. Sat down again. Re-lit her cigarette and coughed slightly. The phone shrilled and she jumped. One ring. She waited. Two rings. She picked it up nervously.

"Hello?"

"Miz Poole, please," said a woman in a snotty voice.

"This is she," Cynthia said politely, taking a drag.

"Good afternoon, Miz Poole. This is Stella Burger calling on behalf of Mr. Jerome's."

Cynthia stifled a giggle. Stella *Burger?*

"Why yes, Miz Burger. I've been expecting your call."

"Yes, well, Miz Poole, Mister Jerome has asked me to ask you if you'll attend an audition, a private screening if you will, where himself will be present. Could that be arranged, Miz Poole?"

"Why, of course Miz Burger, I'd be delighted. When does Mr. Jerome want to see me?"

"Actually Miz Poole, he has an opening, if you will, later this afternoon at Studio A in Deep Cove on the north shore. Would it be possible, at such short notice, for you to attend in a couple of hours from say, this time?"

Cynthia struggled to maintain her composure. Deep Cove? How appropriate. And what planet is this woman from anyway?

"Yes Miz Burger, I'll be sure to make it. I have the address. Is there anything I should bring or wear?"

Miz Burger snorted.

"No, Miz Poole, just some lingerie under whatever you normally wear. Mister Jerome wants to see yourself, not your clothes. We have wardrobe people for that sort of thing."

"Fine, Miz Burger. Thanks so much for calling and you can tell Mr. Jerome I'll see him shortly."

Click. Click.

Cynthia couldn't contain herself any longer and started to giggle. What kind of a bird was that? Miz Burger, my butt. She caressed the phone in its cradle and with a final clickety click of her nails on the receiver, she spun around and danced into the living room. *Mr. Jerome! Mr. Jerome! I'm on my way, Mr. Jerome!* Cynthia Poole danced into her bedroom and started rifling through her lingerie drawers, tossing naughty garter belts, filmy stockings, sheer panties, corsets, bras, teddies, and slips onto her bed. Stripping off her robe, she stood naked in front of her full-length mirror, holding each item up to herself for inspection. White? No, too virginal. Black? Too predictable. Red? Too whorish. Hmmm. Gold? She held up a set of sheer burnished gold-coloured panties and skimpy push-up bra. Yes. They set off her hair perfectly and looked classy and rich. She decided on a black garter belt with the gold underthings and black high-heeled pumps. A black velvet choker snapped quickly around her neck and sheer black stockings with barely discernible golden threads running through them slid smoothly up her legs. Perfect. She smiled at herself in the mirror. Jerome had way more class than old Cecil French, the fat bastard, so she wanted to wear a dress that was on the conservative side but screamed power slut. Cynthia chose a simple black two-piece suit, a short tight skirt with a cinched-in jacket and plunging neckline. She didn't bother with a blouse, liked the way her breasts struggled against each other beside the severely cut lapels. She quickly put her hair up in a long roll with wisps of the blondest bits escaping in a careless but exact plan. Not too heavy on the make-up, red lips, a touch of black eyeliner sweeping up at the corners in tiny ticks, real hair false eyelashes, and a hint of blush. Cynthia stood back and examined the finished product. A pair of simple diamond studs, and she was ready for business.

Today Mr. Jerome. Tomorrow, Hollywood.

Grabbing her purse, she skipped out the door and hailed a taxi. Settling in the back, she lit a smoke and absently scratched her palm with her finger-nails. It was itchy. Cynthia dimly remembered that an itchy palm meant something. She thought it might mean that she would be coming into money. Well, that would make sense. She looked at the harbinger of wealth more closely. She must be more nervous than she first thought. She had actually scratched some of the skin off her palm. *Shit!* She grabbed some cream from her bag and smoothed it on, then covered the redness with a bit of foundation. Satisfied, she clasped her hands and sat up straight, looking directly ahead. Deep Cove, here we come, she thought. My big break. She was so caught up in her imaginings, she didn't even notice her palm still itched.

IX

☞ WHEREIN NATHAN ATTENDS A SWANK PARTY AND
SOME NEW ACQUAINTANCES ARE INTRODUCED.

It had been a couple of months since Nathan Swan
last visited the downtown eastside and he could feel
himself getting anxious again. Out of remission . . .

INITIAL SYMPTOMS: Hypersensitivity, tremor, blurred
vision, lightheadedness, nausea, malaise, verti-
go, insomnia, palpitations, disorientation.

POSSIBLE SYMPTOMS IF LEFT UNTREATED: Acute psy-
chosis, severe convulsions, shock, circulatory
collapse, death.

TREATMENT: Spank the monkey. Choke the chicken.
Get a life.

CONTRAINDICATIONS TO TREATMENT: No reports of
known overdosage have occurred.

After Tawny, the sweet little skull job, he had
stocked up on different pills designed to kill his sex
drive. But as Nathan discovered, what doesn't kill it,

makes it stronger. The beast was again straining against the confines of his better judgment. He had grown weary of his medical texts with deformities and anomalies, his monster skin books. Sure, the conjoined twins, suppurative boils, and crab-infested eyelids still got him hard. But he needed new material. He imagined it was the same with *normal* men and their *normal* magazines. Surfing the net brought some relief, but it was tiresome work to discover just the right site. He felt his options were running out and still, every time he tried to get Big Boy up for a pretty woman, the bastard would fold on him. It just wasn't having anything to do with *normal.*

His colleagues were always inviting him to dinners and clubs. And not wanting to appear an outsider, Nathan had accepted in the beginning. But after a few months of socializing, the questions started. At first, they were easy to answer.

"Are you bringing a date, Nathan? I just want to know so I can figure out the place settings."

"No, Lydia, I'll be coming solo."

Not a problem. But they got trickier to dodge.

"If you're not seeing anyone, I have a girlfriend . . . "

"Thanks, Rachel, but blind dates make me nervous."

Okay, most people understand that. But then, they started getting into dangerous territory. The serious sit-down chats. The *mind your own fucking business* chats.

"Nathan, tell me if I'm out of line here, but . . . "

Or, "Hey buddy, Roxanne's been asking about you. How come you haven't called her?"

Painful dinner parties aside, Nathan's absence at the gyms and squash courts was also noticed.

Pleading weak lungs, carpal tunnel syndrome, and any other medical condition he could think of, Nathan hoped he put those queries to rest.

A couple of times he had joined his counterparts at a strip club, just to fit in, but it was near impossible not to hide his revulsion and the exercise became too dangerous. *Sorry, not my kind of peeler bar, pal.* He assumed everyone might be thinking he was gay, which was a far more preferable alternative to the truth, but Nathan didn't want to start getting set up on dates with men. He had enough to deal with, without making that charade fly.

He had managed this far to alleviate his symptoms with magazines and books and prostitutes. But the attacks were becoming resistant to medication and his preferred modes of relief. Being the good doctor he was, Nathan had sat up nights drinking and chainsmoking and trying to figure out what to do about his situation. He was completely clinical about it. At one point in his musings, and halfway through a bottle of single-malt, he had horrified even himself with a possibility.

What if the next step is stalking and raping women? What if I become a Jack the Ripper of beautiful women?

He had pondered that seriously, leave nothing unexamined. Would that relieve the curse? Maybe he could only get it up for them if they were in a state of terror. Maybe a power trip, asserting his masculinity. Force them to notice him. Force them to take all of him. They wouldn't be laughing then, he thought. And if he became a serial rapist or killer, even the men would fear his presence in their midst. He had taken another gulp of Scotch and walked around the room, playing it out. Maybe, just maybe, he could actually kill women with his penis. How ironic. The source of his weakness, his sickness, could become his supreme power. *Supercock.* He paced some more. He never had discovered what happened to that bitch Marianne Wedge. She had quickly been shipped off somewhere. Maybe he had killed her that night. Internal organ damage, hemorrhaging, whatever. He wondered.

He considered the implications, an exercise mind you, but with half an eye on the big guy to see if it responded. He took it out of his pants and held it, pointing it up to his face.

What do you think, huh? Is that what you want?

But the thick, long member of his own personal congregation did not stand up and shout *Amen, brother!* Nathan realized then, and not without great relief, that he was not saved. He stuffed supercock back into his pants and had another drink. Although he was pleased he would not have to case out model shoots for victims, it still left him staring into the proverbial abyss. This utter emptiness, fruitless struggle to conform, and now, now his preferred crutches were turning on him. Beating him up. What was left, he wondered. What am I missing?

All of which was why Dr. Nathan Swan was found sipping a dry gin martini the following evening at an impossibly boring cocktail benefit party for the hospital. The plan was to fortify himself with alcohol, see and be seen. Mingle, make appropriate macho comments, and seriously make an effort to flirt with a couple of women. He felt a masochistic bit of hope, but it was all such a load of crap. Sometimes, like tonight, he wondered why he wanted to fit in so desperately. Look at them. The doctors – with wives attached to their sides like some kind of wasted, accessory limb, all shrivelled from lack of use – looked like they'd rather be slicing into a hemorrhoid. The ones with mistresses were checking their Rolexes every half hour. And the single ones were pitiable. Drinking too quickly, talking too loudly. Buxom nurses wiggling around the young, single residents, wearing shocking colours, relieved to be out of their bland, constricting uniforms, and taking advantage of the event to display their bedside manner. Most of the residents were from other countries, looking somewhat befuddled and lacking in English language skills, but the Canadian nurses were willing to teach them some foreign tongue. Nathan had even deluded himself into thinking that tonight he might find a female specimen he was attracted to. Better to fit in and be miserable, he supposed, than be a miserable outcast. Why couldn't I have been a fucking poet?

So here he was, in the overdone elegant private club, clutching his martini to his chest. His pacemaker. Although his drink of choice gleamed invitingly on the bar, lovely amber nectar, Nathan knew better than to indulge. He would only get drunk and pissed off. He hated gin, had done since he was a teenager. A martini would go down slowly and he could keep what was left of his wits, securely in check. He circled the room, nodding, smiling like a corpse with rigor mortis, raising his glass in mock camaraderie, gritting his teeth, feeling his bowels spasm, his stomach tighten. His mouth tasted like metal mixed with blood, not entirely unpleasant. He savoured anything uncomfortable to keep him alert. A sharp thwack on his left shoulderblade made his head rock and his glasses slip down his nose. *Be careful what you wish for.*

"Finally decided to get out of your office, huh?"

Taking a deep breath, Nathan turned to see Dr. Malcolm Mueller beaming at him. Mac Mueller, gastroenterologist, *The Mule.* Looked like he had just applied a new coat of black spray-on hair to his bald spot. The rest of his hair, bearing a striking resemblance to an oil slick casualty, was cropped severely in drill-sergeant fashion. The Mule towered over Nathan. True to his moniker, he brayed rather than spoke, and Nathan smelled something sour in Mac's breath now, like death wafting up from his gut. A year-long tan couldn't hide the red spider veins tracking his once-chiselled face, a map leading directly to his liver. The Mule was notorious for fucking around on his wife who, presumably, was the lumpy, short woman at his side. Nathan scrounged around and dug up a hearty grin, stuck out his hand, prepared to have his metacarpals crushed.

"Yeah, they let me out for good behaviour."

Mac Mueller's grip demolished Nathan's hand. Mac's big motherfucking paw, with its fat fingers that had been up his patients' assholes all day. Nathan didn't want to think about it and turned to smile at The Wife.

"Mrs. Mueller, it's nice to finally meet you."

"Please, call me Ruth," said the shapeless sack of flesh from a hole in her face.

"Ruth," Nathan acknowledged, bowing slightly and laying a light kiss on her age-spotted pork chop of a hand, feeling rather pleased with himself.

"Hey, cut that out, Swan!" boomed Mac. "You're gonna make me look bad."

Ruth removed her hand more daintily than Nathan would have thought possible, and she tittered. Nathan liked that. He looked at her more closely and realized that underneath all that primer on her face, she wasn't even blushing. In fact, wasn't that a nasty sidelong glance she was shooting at good old Mac? Bravo. Nathan thought about having an affair with her. Give the drill sergeant doctor a taste of his own medicine. But Mac was diverting things back to himself.

"Nathan here, he's a dermatologist, Ruthie. One of our top skin guys."

Ruthie nodded, staring at Nathan over the rim of her frighteningly orange drink.

"Hell, he's the guy who removed that freakin' mole I had on my butt last year. Remember that, Ruthie? Hell, how could you miss it, it was like a third cheek."

Ruthie's eyes glazed over as she sucked back the day-glo concoction, nodding aimlessly, brownish lipstick marks on the straw. Nathan was fascinated. He remembered Mueller getting the mole removed.

"Shit Swan, can you get this beastly thing off my arse? I've got a date with this Trauma nurse in a week."

Nathan sipped his martini, trying to block out the image of Mueller's silver-haired butt. Ruthie spoke now, releasing her straw.

"Yes, thank you Dr. Swan. We were all very worried it might have been malignant," she said, staring hard at Nathan.

"Call me Nathan," he said, correctly interpreting her meaning.

Hey boys and girls! We're in Opposite Land tonight! Let's play!

"Yes Mrs. Mueller, uh Ruth, it was a nasty piece of business but we were all relieved to discover it was benign."

Ruthie nodded and sucked, and was that a tiny grin turning up the corners of her brown lips? Mac threw back the last of his bourbon and smacked Nathan on the shoulder again.

"Hell Swan, I'm too much of a prick to get the Big C. With my luck, I'll die of old age and keep all my colleagues out of business."

"Let's hope so, Mac," Nathan said from Opposite Land.

"Well, come on Ruthie," Mac said with a touch of slur. "Looks like we're ready for more lubrication."

Draining her glass with a noisy suck, Ruthie again nodded to Nathan.

"Very nice to meet you Nathan."

"Likewise Ruth, hope to see you again."

With that, they turned and began elbowing their way to one of many portable bars. Nathan watched them go. *Lubrication.* He pictured Mueller lubing up a long, weighted, red rubber bougie and shoving it mercilessly down some poor patient's throat to open it up. Choking, sputtering, vomiting, the gag reflex kicking in big time. Or lubing up his sigmoidoscope or any number of medieval looking instruments and eyeing up his patients' puckered assholes with the poor buggers perched on all fours on his examining table, trembling with abject terror. He imagined The Mule would show no mercy there either. *Now, this ain't gonna hurt a bit, just breathe deep, and relax.* Then whammo. Up the old poop chute, baby. Nathan idly wondered what Mueller did with all the hottie nurses he claimed to have scored. Could he only get it up for a good ass drilling? Was Nathan not so different after all? He plucked another martini off a tray that floated past his face and mused. Wouldn't that be something if every doctor could only get aroused by his specialty. To pass the time, he ticked them off in his mind. Neurologists would get erections thinking about doing women in wheelchairs. Pulling their skirts over their heads, lifting their lifeless legs up and spreading them open, hanging them off the chair's arm rests. Pounding into them while the chair spins crazily around the room, wheels squeaking. Neurologists would probably like amnesiacs too. They'd forget things, like maybe the fact that they just blew them an hour ago. Respirologists would get turned on by asthmatics, watching them take a big hit off their inhalers and then wheeze all over their dicks, or better yet, women plugged into ventilators, the *hiss* keeping time with the thrusts. Urologists would, naturally, jerk off to golden showers, and podiatrists would get instant boners fantasizing about women's swollen, misshapen feet. They'd ram those bad boys in their mouths, sucking hungrily, their teeth scraping calloused bunions, clicking on blackened toenails, tongues probing between webbed toes.

Nathan, almost reluctantly, was beginning to enjoy himself at this hellish soiree. It had been some time since he had been able to amuse himself. He wondered about the goons in the morgue, the forensic pathologists, even undertakers. You didn't have to be a doctor to imagine they were all necrophiliacs. Spilling your life seed into a dead body, now *that* was sick. Nathan felt much better now. He glanced across the crowd and the faces and bodies and voices weren't so annoying. Selecting a few young women, he watched them closely, inwardly monitoring his response. He was off to a good start. At least he wasn't feeling panicky and could even bring himself to let his eyes travel their womanly curves without recoiling. It wasn't lust, but it was a beginning. He felt hopeful, maybe martinis were a good thing. The only thing that could send this experiment spiralling back into the petri dish would be if a burn victim waltzed in and put all these lovelies to shame. Jesus, even picturing that made his pants leap erratically. Concentrate, dammit. Over there, by the grand piano, *look at her, you sick fuck.*

So he did. She looked like Jessica Rabbit. Poured into a red backless gown, leaning over on the piano, chin in hands, auburn hair rolling around her head and down her neck and back to where her bra strap would be if she were wearing one. A chunky diamond bracelet grabbed her delicate wrist and the slice up the back of her dress revealed legs custom-made to be some guy's belt. He examined her back and saw a pale rose-coloured birthmark. *Stirring down below.* He still hadn't seen her face. Wouldn't it be delicious if she turned around and had an empty, hollow eye socket. *Hippity hop.* Hell, he sipped his martini and thought, even a nice cleft palate would be pleasant. By picturing a gruesome face, he could actually get down to enjoying the back of her shapely body, something he hadn't done in years. Years. His eyes slid off her shoulderblades, skipped over the birthmark, but his inner eye visualized reptile skin. Couldn't help it. *Ignition.* He paused at her buttocks, round and fleshy, and pictured strips of skin, like the aftermath of a thorough lashing, waving seductively in the breeze from the fan. *We have lift off.*

"Excuse me."

Startled, Nathan blinked and looked down. Shit, it was her. How the fuck did she get over here like that? He looked back to the piano but sure enough, she was gone. And apparently, here she was.

"I'm sorry, but I couldn't help noticing you had been staring at me," she said, her voice low. "I was watching you in the mirror."

Nathan gulped. Tossed back the last of his martini, trying to reconcile his fantasy of Leper Lady with this divine creature obviously sent to test him.

"I'm, uh, sorry miss," he stammered. "I didn't mean to stare, my mind was elsewhere."

"I don't think so," she said, staring directly at his crotch.

Although the freak was behaving now, how was this poor deluded nymphet to know that. Even at its most flaccid, it made quite the impressive package if one were to scrutinize it closely. Even with the front pleats. Ignoring her mesmerized stare, Nathan looked around for a waiter, a gun, anything.

"I'm Nathan Swan," he said, trying to divert her attention. "What brings you to this event?"

She wrenched her gaze up and gave him a wry smile, as if they shared some secret joke or something. Introduced herself as Jane Keller, PR flak for the charity auction occurring later that evening. Then she did an amazing thing. Both hands fluttered back behind her head where – simultaneously – and without looking over her shoulder, she snatched two martinis off another disembodied floating tray. Sipping one, she handed the other to Nathan, never taking her eyes off his. Dumbfounded at her sleight of hand, he accepted with grudging respect. But she wasn't finished with him.

"So tell me, Mr. Swan," she drawled, leaning in. "What was it you found so interesting about me that had your eyes devouring my backside?"

Nathan felt flushed and uncomfortable.

"Well, Miss Keller, um, actually I was looking at your, uh, your birthmark."

Fuck, shit, what a stupid thing to say!

He hastened to redeem himself.

"Sorry, I should introduce myself. I'm actually *Doctor* Swan and I'm a dermatologist. I hope I haven't insulted you, I'm afraid it's a hazard of the job."

But nothing fazed Jane Keller, PR flak. She just tossed her cache of auburn wealth and laughed throatily.

"Oooh! *Doctor* Swan, is it? My apologies."

She sidled up beside him and laid a hand lightly on his upper thigh.

"I have another birthmark, you know," she breathed into his ear, standing on tiptoes. "A much more disgusting one that might interest you deeply. It's dark brown and I believe it even has little hairs growing out of it."

"Hmm, really? How big is it?" Nathan asked, flailing.

"Well doctor," she sighed. "I was thinking maybe you should take a look at it. Don't you even want to know where it is?"

Okay, what the fuck is going on here? Why is the most gorgeous woman here coming on to me?

It was starting up again. Nathan was starting a slow burn. Who was behind this obvious set-up? Was Jane Keller, PR flak, just having her own bit of fun at his expense? Maybe he was mastering the approachable vibe. Maybe she was hammered. Nathan had no illusions about his appearance. Balding, fiftyish, spectacles, nothing spectacular, and usually zero personality in this type of situation. To his knowledge, no one in Vancouver knew about the freak. So who's yanking his chain this time?

"It's somewhere right around here," Jane Keller said slyly, taking his free hand and placing it firmly and squarely on a breast.

He felt her nipple harden under the gauzy material as she moved his hand around in slow circles. Feeling ill, he tried to disengage himself but she had a firm grip and not only on his hand.

"I'll show you mine if you show me yours," she purred, sounding like a voodoo cat.

And her other hand was on his cock in a flash, taking a good exploratory handful. The room tilted. He felt his martini splash onto his arm, and his hand was cringing where she was rotating it on her pumped-up, saline-filled breast. Her eyes were half closed now and she looked sinister, her other hand creeping along his length and breadth. Grabbing, inching, grabbing, inching, martini breath in his face as she looked up at him in acute disbelief.

"My, my, my doctor, what have we got here?" she cackled, long talons invading, probing, searching, and still no end in sight.

She had momentarily released her grip on his breast hand and was slowly shaking her head back and forth, jaw slack, cock hand still foraging in the land of plenty. Nathan availed himself of her stupor to grasp her greedy little paw and remove it from the big guy. Extricating himself from where she'd pinned him to the wall, he sidestepped and handed her his empty glass.

"Nice to have met you, Miss Keller," he said. "I'm afraid I can't stay."

With that, he turned his back and fled the party. The last thing he saw of Jane Keller, PR flak, she was staring at her hand in a trance-like state, like she'd just done a big hit of acid. Assuming correctly that she was a bit of a loose cannon, Nathan felt safe in the assumption that no one would believe her anyway. Because, although Nathan Swan didn't know much about women, that much he did know. She would talk. The big fish story. The one that got away. Racing out onto the street to hail a cab, he started to relax. Poor Jane. He knew how far apart she would be holding her hands when describing his tackle, and he also knew she'd get nary a nibble.

As he settled back in the taxi, he was surprised to discover that he wasn't displeased with the evening. Sure, he still wasn't getting aroused by beauty. The freak had laid dormant all night except for the fantasizing. But, he had accomplished what he had set out to do. He had mingled. He had pulled that much off. Even the PR flak was a wee bit of a victory. He wasn't feeling let down or filled with spite this time. And who could forget Mac and Ruth. The Muellers. That made him smile and smiling felt good, dammit. Why, he had even flirted with the idea of having it off with old Ruthie. He chuckled at that. Out loud! Saw the cabbie's eyes flicker into the rearview for a second. He wouldn't diagnose himself as normal, but tonight for the first time in decades, Nathan Swan felt somewhat happy. How odd.

X

☞ A CREEPING DISFIGUREMENT PROMPTS
CYNTHIA TO QUESTION HER SELF-WORTH.

Cynthia Poole lay on her cold bathroom floor, naked and shivering. She heard someone pounding on her apartment door and yelling. It was Patrick, dear sweet Patrick, and she had been avoiding him for three weeks now. She covered her ears. Patrick could be very persistent, maybe that was one of the things that made her fall in love with him a few months ago. The way he wooed her, the way he didn't care what she did for a living, his oh-so-normal life into which he welcomed and included her, not hiding her away like a trophy or a sin. Cynthia rocked back and forth on her knees, holding her head, eyes squeezed shut. *Please, Patrick, go away! You can't see me like this!*

Finally, the knocking subsided and she could hear his boots thud down the hallway. Cynthia poked her head out from under the sink and looked from side to side. As if someone was watching her. Her hair was matted and filthy, the blonde streaks fading and receding from her crown. Her face was flushed and splotchy from crying and clear snot hung from her nose like a raindrop. She crawled on her hands and knees along the floor and hauled herself up to the sink. Couldn't help it, turned to the full length mirror and stared. It was still true, not a nightmare. She felt like screaming. *What the hell is going on?* Her skin, once flawless, was now shedding, like she was some kind of snake. She looked at her elbows, and with a chipped nail flicked at the skin flakes. A couple of clear bits of skin floated to the tile floor. But things were much worse elsewhere. Turning around, she saw angry erosion behind her knees, red, scaly patches that felt like sharp claws digging into her every time she bent her leg. Leaning over the sink, Cynthia splashed cold water on her swollen face, but couldn't take her eyes off her body. Every day, a new bit of skin fell off and a new crack opened up, oozing liquid. It was spreading like some kind of out-of-control toxic invasion and it was all Cynthia could do to hold her mind together. She had already lost her gig at Jerome's. After her brilliant audition, and one film she was very proud of, Cynthia had felt her career starting to build the way she had planned. But then, this. It had started on her palms, the first sign something was terribly wrong. Cynthia had no experience with imperfection, never having had so much as a zit in adolescence.When she first noticed the dry skin, she flipped out, slapping on hand cream, soaking in baby oil, trying to cover it with make-up. Bad enough she had to look at it. But things quickly worsened, like the time she was in a liquor store buying a bottle of wine. Feeling the cashier's appreciative eyes on her as she bent over in her tight skirt, perusing the wine racks, almost made her forget the condition of her hands. She made her selection and walked to the cash, flirting with her eyes, doing the hair flip thing. She could tell the college kid was flustered and it excited her. He rang in her bottle, and she slid a twenty across the counter, smiling, coy. Cynthia held out her hand for the change, eyes twinkling at him. A moment. A shift. Something was wrong, he wasn't responding. She wasn't holding his gaze, in fact, he was backing off, looking embarrassed and . . . what else? Cynthia blinked and looked down. She could have died. Her hand, held out for the change, palm up, was bleeding. And something that looked like pus was bubbling out. She snatched her hand back, horrified. She couldn't even look at college dude, grabbed her bottle and left the change on the counter. Ran out the door, and jumped on a bus, any bus, the one pulling into the stop outside the liquor store. It was packed. Cynthia pushed her way to the middle, shaken, and the bus lurched away from the curb. Without thinking, she grabbed a pole to steady herself, but by mistake grabbed a woman's hand that was also holding the pole. The woman shrieked, pulled her hand away and rubbed it on her coat, glaring at Cynthia. *Fuck.* She ducked under someone's arm and pushed further back, falling into everyone because her hands were rammed into her pockets, her bottle clutched under an arm. People shoved her back and she stumbled into the stairs at the back exit, quickly whipped out a clenched fist and with one free finger managed to pull the cord for the next stop without attracting any undue attention. Cynthia ran off the bus, hailed a cab home, and paid a seven dollar fare with a twenty.

"Keep the change," she shot over her shoulder as she scurried into her apartment, where she sat for the next two hours cutting the fingers off all her gloves and trying them on.

It was summer. She couldn't very well be wearing full-on gloves, but she had to do something.

From there, it moved to the soles of her feet and if she kept her socks on, no one noticed. But one day, she was wearing white ankle socks, in the middle of a good fucking scene, when Jerome had yelled, CUT!

"What the hell is all over your socks, Cynthia?" he had asked, striding over.

She had looked down and seen dried blood. *No, not again.* Brownish red blood drying on her clean white socks. When she tried to pull her socks off to look, they got stuck on the blood and the pus and she ripped even more skin off. Jerome had blanched and turned his back.

"Get that looked at, young lady, and don't come back until it's cleared up. Whatever the hell it is."

Mortified, Cynthia had hobbled off the set. She had not been back since, and later when she discovered it had crept to her elbows and knees, she went incommunicado. No Patrick, no Jerome, and if she didn't do something about this soon, there would be no Cynthia left. Just a pile of scattered skin.

She had been to her doctor, who appeared to be just as flaky as she was becoming, and he diagnosed her with dermatitis and eczema and everything in between. Try this steroid cream, that coal tar,

71

betamethasone, up-your-ass-a-sone, and heck, why not some ginseng tea while you're at it, honey. Cynthia was alternating between depression and anger and grabbed her most recent cream. An ugly brick-coloured ointment that stained her skin purple when she applied it. She remembered her doctor giving it to her.

"Now, this is the most powerful thing we can give you. It actually comes from an old Indian cure, been around for ages," the geek had said.

"Don't, I repeat, don't have this on for more than twenty minutes at a time. And for maximum bene-fit, wrap plastic bags around your feet and hands after you apply it. But don't leave it on longer than twenty minutes or it might just burn your skin right off!"

Cynthia smirked as she slathered the strong-smelling stuff on her hands and feet now. *Hah! The way I'm starting to look, I wouldn't mind burning all my skin off and just starting fresh again, thank you very much.*

She had been painting her hands and feet in this shit for weeks now, wrapping them up tight in little baggies, and sleeping all night like that. It hadn't worked. Either way. She smoothed new, clean plastic on her hands and feet now in preparation for bed. One more night, she decided. One more night, and that's it. I'm getting the geek to refer me to a specialist. Crawling painfully between her sheets, carefully so as not to dislodge the baggies, Cynthia lay still. Her eyes filled up and she sniffled again. What had happened? Everything was going so well. It was so, so difficult finding a decent guy in this business who loved you for who, not what, you were. She smiled a tiny smile, thinking about Patrick. But then, she moved and her foot split open again. What kind of sex life would they have with this. She was a monster, and he was a god. *Gods and monsters.* Cynthia thought she recalled a movie by that title and wondered what it had been about. No, she loved Patrick too much to subject him to this. Because Patrick, she knew, would deal with it. He wouldn't say anything, he'd go along and be supportive, but she would see it in his eyes. She would hear it in his voice. Pity. Or worse, horror. He was so proud of her when they went out together. She would hang off his strong arm, gazing adoringly into his eyes, and everyone would see how much they were in love. How could he love her now? Shit, even she couldn't love herself and she was her greatest fan.

She rolled over cautiously onto her side and stared at the wall. She made shadow puppets like she used to do. When mummy had gone to heaven and she was alone in the house with daddy. The counsellor had taught her that. Dancing girls were her favourite and she tried to do them now, but the bags got in the way and it was too painful to hold her arms up. And what about her career? Just when things were happening with Jerome, a few short flicks and a feature nearly ready to wrap. She knew from the day of the audition they were sympatico. She had knocked his socks off that day. Now, he had knocked hers off, dried blood and all.

Thinking of all she had lost, her man, her gig, and half her fucking epidermis, Cynthia Poole fell into a troubled sleep. As she slept, her little bagged hands and feet curled into fetal-like creatures, her skin slowly evolving to a deeper shade of purple at the same rate as the darkening sky. The purple sky that Cynthia Poole had once wanted to eat. Stars and all.

BOOK TWO
The Fun House

THINGS TAKE AN UNEXPECTED TURN FOR
CYNTHIA AND NATHAN, WHO ARE THROWN
TOGETHER THROUGH CIRCUMSTANCES BEYOND
THEIR CONTROL. THIS UNEASY ALLIANCE FORCES
THEM TO CONFRONT THEIR FEARS AND FAILINGS
AND RE-EVALUATE THEIR SELF-WORTH. CONCERNING
WHAT HAPPENS WHEN BEAUTY BECOMES THE
BEAST. LIKE A HALL OF MIRRORS, NOTHING IS
WHAT IT SEEMS.

I

⌒ CONCERNING THE INITIAL MEETING OF THE TWO
MAIN CHARACTERS IN THE FLESH; NATHAN'S DÉJÀ
VU AND SUBSEQUENT REALIZATION.

Bobby Brightman had just left Dr. Swan's office. His acne was improving, and his step was jauntier than when he had first begun treatment. Nathan smiled to himself as the door shut behind the Brightman boy. He was a good kid, and Nathan was pleased. In the past month, Bobby had picked up the guitar and along with it, a girlfriend. Shit, maybe he should learn guitar himself, Nathan thought. Soothe his savage breast. Physician, heal thyself, and all that crap. Although he still suffered his spells, he tried not to dwell on them as much. Just keep away from temptation and don't encourage anxiety-provoking situations. Control, control, control.

"Dr. Swan? Your one o'clock is here."

Nathan leaned over the intercom.

"Thank you Marjorie, I'll be right with you."

He picked up the chart, a thin chart, new patient. Flipped through it, Cynthia Marie Poole. Twenty years old. Not much information thus far. Letter from her referring GP. Differential diagnoses: ? dermatitis, eczema, psoriasis. Various meds tried to nil effect. He scratched his head diffidently and buzzed Marjorie.

"Send her in, please."

He heard the door close, and head bent down writing, he motioned her in with one arm.

"Come on in, Miss Poole, have a seat."

Silence. He looked up, squinting, to see her still standing by the door. She was wearing a big floppy hat, large sunglasses, and gloves. She wasn't moving, gripping a purse tightly with both hands. Nathan put his pen down and gave her a smile.

"Miss Poole? Come on in, please."

She tentatively stepped closer to his desk, skittish, nervous. Nathan frowned slightly. Shit, not another one of these beautiful, empty-headed cover girls with a nasty rash from rugburn or something. The jumpy one finally reached his desk and gracefully lowered herself into the opposite chair.

"I'm Doctor Swan," Nathan said, rising from his chair a few inches. "And you must be Cynthia Poole. I see Dr. Lasky referred you. You've been having some problem with your skin? Why don't you tell me about it."

Cynthia Poole nodded and first removed her big hat. Her luxurious hair tumbled from it in a rush of brown and dull blonde and a shower of dead skin. She shook her head slightly, an affect still with her, despite the flurry of cells. Then Cynthia Poole removed her large sunglasses and looked Dr. Swan right in the eyes. Her own eyes were blue, but a little red and puffy around the edges despite her obvious attempts at concealment. A very beautiful woman, he noted with clinical detachment and a vague sense of unease. Next, she removed her gloves, one finger at a time, daintily and with precision. Nothing so far. Nothing he could see, so he waited, leaning back in his chair. Then Cynthia Poole leaned closer and slapped both hands on his desk, palms up. Aha. Here we go. Leaning forward, Nathan took each hand and examined it closely, lightly touching the scales and asking questions. Cynthia relaxed a bit. He didn't seem as clueless as Dr. Lasky. After all, this was his specialty, wasn't it.

"Anywhere else?" he asked simply.

Cynthia nodded and took off her jacket. Underneath she was wearing a plain white sleeve-less blouse and she displayed her elbows to the good doctor. Getting up from behind his desk, Nathan came around and carefully took each elbow, gently turning them and brushing them with his fingers. He smiled benignly at her now.

"And? How about the backs of your knees? Action there as well?"

Cynthia managed a shy smile and raised an eye-brow at him. Lifting her skirt above her knees, she showed him the latest patches of diseased skin. Nathan kneeled down and again put a practised hand to the sore spots, asking a few questions.

"I'm guessing the soles of your feet are a bit of a mess then, aren't they?" he said, returning to his desk.

When Cynthia bent down to remove a pump, he waved his hand.

"No need to show me right now, we'll take a prop-er look in the exam room later, but I think I can tell you right now that you most definitely have psoriasis."

Cynthia let out some breath she had been holding in. Psoriasis. She had heard of it, but thought it was just like really bad dandruff. *Heartbreak of psoriasis.* On the one hand, she was relieved. At least this guy seemed capable and sure of himself. Maybe now she could get on with treatment and her life.

Nathan asked her to tell him about her history. Her psoriatic history, that is. Beginning with the first time she noticed that itch on her palm in the taxi, up until now. Where, when, how, and what. The more you tell me, the more I can help you, the good doctor had said. So, Cynthia Poole spoke at length for the first time in weeks. It was such a relief to talk again, to tell someone. As she prattled on about this scab and that scale and this flake and that fluid, she became more animated and moved around in her chair. Nathan was watching her closely, at first for signs of depression or anxiety, as many patients were prone to suffer with this disease. But the more he watched her flip her hair about, or knit her brow a certain way, or flash her teeth just so, the more he felt he'd seen her before. Whenever she'd pause, he'd smile and wave her on.

"No, please, go on. The more I know, the better."

And Cynthia, starved for human discourse, eagerly picked up the thread and exorcised some of her pain through discussion of her tormentor that now had a name. Psoriasis The Horrible. Nathan narrowed his eyes and searched his memory. He had seen her before, he was sure of it. But where?

"And then, I tried those stupid baggies and that weird medication . . . "

Was she at that benefit party, he wondered. No, he didn't think so. Was she a nurse on staff at the hospital. No, that would have been in her chart.

"But I wore them all night long anyway, and nothing happened . . . "

Think man, think. It was driving him crazy. It wasn't her voice, he was sure he hadn't heard it before. It was her face and her body. He sat up straighter. Yes, her body. And then he did something he never did with patients, especially beautiful ones. He tried to picture her naked. And as she rattled away, he divested her of her blouse, her brassiere and her skirt. Yes! He wiped the remaining blonde from her hair, and nearly had it. There was just one thing different. Her eyes, he thought. What if they were green? And then he had it and sucked in his breath so sharply, Cynthia stopped talking and looked at him questioningly. Or rather, Charity Heatherton looked at him. He quickly put her clothes back on and re-focused on what she was saying.

"Go on, you were telling me about the troubles you're having with walking lately."

Cynthia nodded hesitantly, sensing something had shifted, but so eager to talk she just jumped back in. Nathan let out a long breath. Charity-fucking-Heatherton, sure enough. A few years older, but it's definitely that cunt from *Playboy*. How interesting. Wonder what she does for a living now? He couldn't wait to get to the history taking. *Oh, you're an accountant? Tell me, are spreadsheets much different than spreading your legs for horny men? Oh, and by the way, if you don't mind me asking, can you just get the fuck out of my office? You never helped me, why should I help you?*

I I

 ⟡ CYNTHIA'S CHART.

NAME: Cynthia Marie Poole, *aka Charity-fucking-Heatherton*

AGE: Twenty.

DOB: May 15, 1979

BIRTHPLACE: Vancouver, B.C.

STATUS: Single, no dependents.

PAST MEDICAL HISTORY: Typical childhood illnesses, tonsillectomy, broken ankle, nil else of note.

FAMILY HISTORY: No siblings. Parents deceased. No history of psoriasis in the family.

PAST SURGICAL HISTORY: Corrective ankle surgery, extensive orthodontic work. *Abortion, I'd be willing to bet.*

PERSONAL HISTORY: Born in Vancouver, single, lives alone. Currently employed as a model, on disability due to illness. *Lets men put their dicks inside her for money. Note: probably gives great blowjobs.*

HISTORY: First signs of scaling noted about three months ago. Steady, rapid multiplying of skin cells. Now evident on hands, feet, elbows, knees, plaque

82

type with some pustular. *Basically, this chick's going to be a fine mess, 'cause we all know there's no cure.*

PHYSICAL EXAM: Vitals BP 125/80, heart rate 75 per minute, chest clear, lung fields clear, height five-foot-seven, weight 120 pounds, CNS exam normal, musculoskeletal exam normal, GI and GU exams normal. *Nice tits, great ass, but a whole lot of freakin' ugly psoriasis scabbing up nicely and messin' with her mind. Too bad, 'cause she's SUCH a pretty gal.*

ECG: Normal.

BLOODWORK: Normal.

REFLEXES: Normal. *Gag.*

CONCLUSION: Psoriasis, man. No cause. No cure.

III

☞ RELATES TREATMENT OPTIONS FOR CYNTHIA'S CONDITION AND HER REACTION TO SUCH.

Nathan had a hard time separating Cynthia Poole from Charity Heatherton each time she was in his office. It was pissing him off, but each time she came in, she was worse. And the scalier she got, the better she started to look to Nathan. They were at the point now, where he was recommending UVB treatments. Cynthia freaked.

"Radiation? Are you fucking crazy? Isn't there any kind of pill I can take?"

"It's the only option left, Cynthia," Nathan said, feeling unsettled. "Look, your skin cells are multiply-ing at an abnormally fast rate. That's what psoriasis is. The cells are producing so fast, that they're falling all over each other and shedding uncontrollably."

Cynthia sniffed.

"I'm not an idiot. You already told me all that, Dr. Swan."

She turned, her poor face now starting to peel around the edges of her ears.

84

"Look doc, bad enough my skin is falling off, but if I have to walk around bald, wearing some stupid kerchief on my head, I'd rather die."

Nathan shook his head.

"Cynthia, it's not like chemo, although I won't say there aren't potential side effects. The UVB treatments are just ultraviolet light. You know, like the part of the sun that actually burns you. Sometimes, those rays will slow down the rapid growth of your skin cells."

She slumped in a chair.

"Sometimes?"

Nathan nodded.

"And my hair won't fall out?"

"No."

Nathan could understand. Her hair was her final vanity. But he had to be clear.

"There is no cure, Cynthia. But UV treatments have been effective for some patients. Look, you really don't have much choice. Nothing else is working."

She looked at him.

"What if the UV treatments don't work? Then what?"

Nathan felt like saying, then I refer you to the suicide counselling room. But he didn't.

"Your psoriasis could just disappear at any time for no apparent reason. There's always hope. We don't really know everything about this disease."

Cynthia wrung her pitiful hands out of habit, but they immediately cracked open and bled. Nathan hurried over with a compress and wrapped her palms loosely. She looked at him with gratitude.

"I don't know how much more of this I can take,"

she said, watching him bent over her hands. "Do you have any idea, any idea at all, how much this is screwing up my life? And now you're telling me I have to get my skin burnt off with some radiation, some UVB crap, that might not even work, and then what? Then you give up?"

Nathan didn't know what to say. As a doctor, he felt sorry for her. She was suffering, perhaps more than his other patients. From what he could gather, both Cynthia's social and professional lives revolved around her looks. Not that Nathan found that hard to believe. *Welcome to the real world, honey. How's it feel?*

But as a man, he felt a sense of retribution. She was Cathy, the cheerleader, his first real crush at the new high school. Cathy who had pretended to like him and lured him into the gym one night with promises of *doing it*. The darkened gym where she had pulled his pants down, and then the lights had all blazed at once, and the stands were full of jeering, leering teenagers. She was Megan, fellow med school student, who recoiled in horror. Maybe because she was going to specialize in gynecology and just couldn't wrap her brain around the logistics. And finally, she was his mother, who spent hours sweating over her sewing machine, trying to fashion invisible panels into his blue jeans, when tight jeans were in style.

But now, she was his patient.

"So, what do I have to do for these treatments, Dr. Swan?"

He motioned her to sit and gave her a pamphlet explaining the treatments and directions to the Skin Care Centre. He explained how, because she had psoriasis invading all parts of her body, she would have to stand in a tall enclosed tube for short blasts of the ultraviolet rays to her entire body.

"You mean like a stand-up sun bed?"

"I suppose something like that, but you have to cover your face and, uh, genitals."

"Will I at least get a tan out of the deal?"

Against his better judgment, Nathan laughed, and silently berated himself. *Consorting with the enemy!*

"You'll get the best tan you've ever had Cynthia, and all at the province's expense."

She smiled a bit at that.

"I've never had a tan you know. I've always tried to stay out of the sun and protect my skin. Kinda ironic, huh?"

Their appointment nearly over, just an information session on the UV treatments, Cynthia turned to leave. But before she got to the door, Nathan surprised himself and called her back.

"Have you had any new lesions since our last visit?"

Cynthia furrowed her brow and then her eyes widened and she pulled her sweater out of her pants. Holding it up with one hand, she pulled the waistband of her jeans down slightly with the other. Nathan bent over and inspected her flat tummy with its sparkly little navel ring winking at him. A new crop of blisters had sprung up around her belly button. He frowned. The disease was spreading.

"I suppose I'm going to have to take my ring out," she said.

Nathan stepped back for another look and shook his head. Just when he was starting to empathize, she would set him back again with a show of vanity.

"No, if you want to keep it in, it's fine for now."

"Well, that's something, I guess," Cynthia said, pulling her sweater back down. "Not that I'll be parading around in a bikini any time soon."

He opened the door for her.

"I'll see you after your first session with the UVB, okay? You can let me know how it went."

Cynthia flashed one of her rare smiles at him. It took him by surprise and his stomach actually lurched at its bravery.

"Thanks doc, see ya next week with my new tan lines."

IV

☞ IN WHICH NATHAN AGAIN TAKES HIMSELF IN
HAND; A NEW EXPERIMENT WITH SURPRISING
AND DELIGHTFUL RESULTS.

It had been several weeks since Cynthia had
started her treatments in the tube. Aside from
showing signs of tanning, the only other evidence of
change was not good news. Nathan noticed she was
getting increasingly agitated at their visits and slipping into what could become a severe depression if
left unchecked. She didn't go anywhere now without her hat, glasses and gloves, and had taken to
wearing turtleneck long-sleeved sweaters and baggy
skirts that fell to her ankles. Her hair was almost
back to its original brown, but lack of attention had
left it dull and clumped. Although initially she had
been almost excited about the UVB treatments, she
had now regressed to monosyllabic conversation
and had an unnerving habit of picking at her skin
and opening it up afresh. Nathan was talking to her
more now, trying to get her to react to the real world
and her surroundings but with little effect. She was

losing her bravado, and the less she spoke, the harder he tried to draw her out. Patients had been known to give up living with this disease. At one visit, as she idly picked her arm and he quietly removed her hand, giving it a *naughty, naughty* tap, she reminded him of some of the addicts he had seen on his visits to the downtown eastside. Cynthia had told him she never did drugs, a statement he believed, but in her present state she would not have looked out of place sitting on East Hastings Street, peering inside her flesh to see what manner of parasite crawled out. He didn't think she had given up entirely yet, and their appointments were becoming more like simple counselling sessions, but she was on her way to despair. Nathan believed this was probably the first time in her young life that Cynthia had not cared what she looked like. It surprised him that he did not feel malicious about this turn of events. He didn't even feel smug. This rattled him, because the worse she looked, the more he found himself taking extra care in the morning with his appearance. He had even caught himself sucking in his stomach the other day when he stood to greet her. Not that it would have mattered. She barely made eye contact any more. But this new development dismayed him somewhat, and worse, he felt another spell coming on. Odd that, he hadn't had one in awhile.

He stood on his balcony, watching the sun set and sipped his Scotch. The freak was coiled, but jumpy. Nathan was feeling a sense of nervous apprehension mixed with the usual sick feeling that typically preceded a bout. Sweat was beading on his forehead, cooled intermittently with an evening breeze and his hand holding the glass shook slightly. But for the first time, his mind was not completely consumed with the symptoms and inevitable distasteful act of release. Cynthia Poole was in there too somewhere, like an annoying yet endearing child. Her precious feet, chipped polish on her toenails, and a silver toe ring. Hardened soles yellow with pus and dull red with dried blood, and a silvery armour of plaque-like skin that made a *click* sound if you tapped on it with a fingernail. The freak lurched, his guts twisted. After taking a final look at the darkening sky and twinkling lights on the mountains, Nathan returned to the living room. It was coming on quickly this time. His pants were moving and rippling. Soon they would be straining and he would have to unleash it. *Let's just get this over with, shall we?* Forgoing his reclining chair, he headed straight for the office. No time to surf the net, he closed the blinds and selected his favourite textbook. Fumbling with his fly, he unzipped and It flew up, hitting the underside of his desk top with a thud. He grimaced, leafing through the pages of monsters. Hand firmly on the tiller, he readied himself to navigate his way through the pitiful wasteland. A woman with skin like the hide of a rhino beckoned. Nathan settled in, priming the pump. But, the picture blurred on the page and he blinked and realized his hand was still. The freak was fired up and ready, but he was thinking about something else. A half formed idea was taking shape and he paused, trying to sort it out. An experiment, yes. Closing the book on rhino woman, he marched back into the living room with a determined step. The freak was swinging heavily, confused with the unfamiliar

events, but trusting and ready. *Hang in there, mister.*
Nathan scrambled around in his magazines, looking
for the old *Playboy*. He was breathing irregularly,
excitement laced with dread and apprehension.
Come to daddy, Cynthia. Aha! He found the magazine. Not even taking time to sit, he rifled through
the issue like a crazed housewife looking for
coupons. He pawed past Miss January, crumpling
her face in the process. And there she was. Charity
Heatherton in all her sublime perfection. Well, hello
there Miss Poole. The doctor will see you now.
Nathan leaned her up against his bookshelf and still
standing, knees shaking, he took himself in hand.
One. Two. Slowly, now. Easy boy. Charity locked
eyes with him, urging him, helping him. She wanted this as much as he did, he could tell. Even the Big
Boy could sense it. Her green eyes were encourag-
ing, but he saw blue. Faster now, yes, like that. He
felt his soul start to open as the freak swelled and
pulsed with the rhythm of his hand. *Cynthia.*
Smooth, white skin, not a mark anywhere and he
was working it. Amazement as he picked up the
tempo and his dance partner followed, not missing
a beat. Years dropped away. *Faster, my god, we love
this.* He was a teenager again. In his bedroom, under
the blankets, the freak pulsing with guilt-edged
splendour. Fantasies of Marilyn, staring at her
poster. Fantasies of Cynthia, now. A real woman, a
woman he could touch tomorrow if he chose. Going
mad, a breakthrough. A fucking breakthrough!
Hand flying now, no sense of decorum, wild giddi-
ness, head thrown back, not even looking anymore,
can see her with his eyes closed, can see her on the

ceiling, even picture her mouth on his cock and still, the momentum builds. Nothing can stop it now, insufferable sweetness, how long it's been. How much he's missed. It's exquisite, it's too much, it's almost, almost – panting like a dog, grinning – *we're nearly there, Cynthia*, his body splits up the middle and a dark shadow shoots out of him, leaving light and brilliance, a supreme flash, exploding in tiny bits of coloured glass and piano tinkling and searing blindness – but he can see! And great loopy wads of semen fly as Nathan Swan screams out his demons, sinks to the floor and cries like a baby.

V

☞ CYNTHIA EXPERIENCES A TRANSFORMATION
AKIN TO THAT OF A BUTTERFLY'S LIFE CYCLE,
ALBEIT IN REVERSE.

Cynthia Poole is sitting on her bed clutching a photograph, her hand layered with dragon skin. She knows nothing of Dr. Swan's metamorphosis. But her own transformation is rapidly devouring her. Literally eating away at her flesh, flaying back the epidermal layers, laying bare a part of her she had never acknowledged. Cynthia did not understand any of this. The only deep things about Cynthia were the ever-widening fissures snaking across her body. The photograph she is holding is that of Little Miss Vancouver 1983, a pretty girl with brown ringlets and a sparkly crown. She is standing between two grownups, holding their hands. Two tall figures, their faces in shadow. Little Miss is wearing a party dress and her shoes are shined to a high gloss. Her lips are bright red and her eyes are blue. *Three foot two, eyes of blue* . . . Cynthia picks at a scab and clear fluid runs out. She wonders who the girl is. *Has anybody seen my gal?* Picking up the photograph, she holds it inches from her tanned nose and squints at it. What a pretty creature, she thinks. I wonder who owns her? She turns it upside down and something ripples through her memory, but it's gone just as quickly. A long fingernail absently slices open a blister on her tummy and she hums a familiar tune. She studies the girl, struggling to remember. But she can't. A voice hisses in her head. *Get up, get up you little fool.* Cynthia drops the photo as if it's on fire. She gets up. Shaking, disoriented, she walks into the bathroom. Funny, her nerves are bad. Better take some nerve pills. That scary woman in the mirror is looking at her again. Cynthia opens the medicine cabinet. Poof! The woman is gone. She finds the bottle and grasps it tightly. Head bowed to avoid the apparition, Cynthia shuffles into the kitchen leaving smudges of blood on the linoleum. Somebody's mutilated arm reaches into the fridge and grabs a bottle of white wine. *Cyndi, hand me my nerve pills, there's a good girl.* Obediently, Cynthia pours the entire bottle into the strange looking hand. The fist closes over and Cynthia picks up the bottle of wine. She walks, using only her heels, back to the bedroom and sits on the bed. There's a photograph lying there. How did that get there, she wonders. Who's brat is that? Shrugging, Cynthia pours the nerve pills into her mouth. All of them. She feels silly and starts to giggle, a few tablets spitting out. Oops! Grabbing the bottle of wine, Cynthia Poole washes down her medicine. Great gulps, spluttering, choking, cold wine spilling down her naked breasts, stinging her raw skin. She drinks until all the pills are on their way, then sits on the edge of the bed, holding the photograph again, puzzling, and drinking until the entire bottle of wine is gone.

She didn't hear the pounding on her apartment door, the yelling, or the key turning in the lock. Nor did she know her landlord had just barged into the room, angry, with her eviction notice sticking out of his shirt pocket. She didn't hear him say *Shit* as he punched in 911 on her phone.

As the paramedics carried Cynthia Poole out on a stretcher, one of them slipped on the polished floor. Looking down, he carelessly peeled a photograph off the bottom of his shoe and tossed it aside. She didn't see that either.

VI

Nathan is getting ready for work. Looking in the mirror, he straightens his tie, humming a tune. He is not displeased with his image. Maybe it's his eyes, they're happier somehow. Or maybe it's because Cynthia Poole is coming in today. He's brimming with self confidence and hopes he can parlay some of it to his patient. Dabbing on some aftershave, he grins at himself. Actually grins. He had gazed into the abyss and for once, the monster staring back wasn't him. He planned to go out and buy a year's worth of skin books, real skin books, and masturbate himself into a frenzy. He couldn't wait to get out onto the street and look at women. Pretty women. Julia Roberts type women. He was in tune with his body, the freak was perking up even at the thought. Nathan wanted to call all his macho colleagues and go to a strip club, he wanted to rent porno flicks, head down to a peep show, maybe even cruise the downtown south for the classy hookers. The world was his for the taking, and he had Cynthia Poole to thank for it. A final tug on his tie, and he walked into the living room for his briefcase. The phone rang and he turned on his way out the door. He wanted to ignore it, but that not being the lot of a doctor, he set his briefcase down.

"Hello?" he said quickly, impatiently.

And his world collapsed.

She was still alive, miraculously. Nathan looked down at her in the bed and she looked so incredibly fragile. Like a child. Her pallor made the lesions even more frightening and his heart twisted. His patient, his saviour, and he felt so helpless. Nathan pounded his fist against the wall and a perky nurse poked her head in.

"Everything all right, Dr. Swan?" she asked.

"Yes, thank you. Just give me a minute to talk to her."

"She's a very lucky girl," the nurse said, lingering.

Fuck off, you nosy twat!

Nathan nodded his head and glared at her. Stop staring at me like that, he thought. I'm a doctor. You're a nurse. That means I'm better than you. Get it? Now get out. Nurse Busybody withdrew and Nathan turned back to his patient. He clasped one of her mutilated hands. Her fingers felt cold. She moaned and turned her head towards him.

"Cynthia?" he whispered, feeling like shit, like it was somehow his fault.

"It's Doctor Swan. Wake up."

"What?" she croaked, opening one eye a slit and focusing on him. "What are you doing here? Where the fuck am I?"

"You're in the hospital Cynthia, but you're going to be fine."

"What happened?" she said, opening both blue eyes wider.

Nathan shifted uncomfortably.

"Well, we think you accidentally may have taken too many pills last night and passed out. Your landlord found you and called the ambulance. So here you are."

She waved her hand dismissively and struggled to sit up.

"Of course I took too many pills, you idiot. Why am I still alive and wasting my breath talking to you?"

There. Out with it. Just like that. And now that she had admitted it, he wanted to deny it. Vehemently.

"Now, Cynthia, are you sure? Maybe you just had too much wine and lost count of your pills."

She looked at him like he was a stupid child.

"Nice try, doc. I don't actually remember what I was thinking at the time, but I definitely remember planning on pegging out. And the second someone springs me from this dump, I'm going to get it right. Don't tell me that surprises you."

Nathan was shaken. Time for doctor mode.

"Listen Cynthia, you don't know what you're saying. You're a beautiful young woman and you've got your whole life ahead of you. This will clear up eventually. Think about your modelling career, your friends."

An ugly look crossed Cynthia's face and she sat up straighter, her eyes completely clear now.

"Are you a complete idiot? Look at me!"

She ripped the sheet off and struggled with her nightgown trying to untie it but her bandanged hands were giving her trouble.

"Friends? You think I have friends?" she screeched. "I don't have any friends left! I'm a fucking freak!"

Nathan was getting scared, and murmured something, grasping for her flailing hands, trying to keep her from disrobing. They tussled a bit, and Cynthia grew still. He cautiously took his hands away. Her eyes narrowed and she glared at him with something akin to amusement, but it was terrifying. Like a clown gone bad.

"My modelling career," she said quietly. "I don't have a modelling career."

Nathan tried a shaky smile.

"Well, not right now, but you'll get it back again. You've got to give these UV treatments a chance, Cynthia."

She threw her head back and howled with malicious glee. Then snapped her head back and gazed at him levelly.

"You're a joke, doc. I never did have a fucking modelling career. Maybe when I was four or five years old, maybe then. Do you want to know what my so-called career really is? Do you? Do you?"

Nathan sputtered and got a queasy feeling. He didn't want her to know that he knew about the *Playboy* pictures. He had assumed she had moved on from those days and now, was a highly paid model, like she said. Like she said, dammit. He was feeling ill, but there was no stopping her now. She reared up in the hospital bed and lashed out.

"I'm an actress!" she shrieked, tossing her hair. "I'm a fucking actress Doctor Swan, maybe you've seen some of my work!"

This was very confusing to Nathan. What? An actress? That's better than being a model. That's a good thing. Why is she screaming? She can still be an actress, in fact she's doing a pretty good job right now. He cleared his throat, she looked at him, waiting, a sense of triumph in her eyes. Something was amiss, but he couldn't think fast enough. *Okay, I'll play, but I think I'm going to wish I was in Opposite Land.*

"What movies were you in, Cynthia?"

The key had turned. The second the words escaped his mouth, he knew he'd made a mistake. She was going to open this box, and he wasn't going to like it.

"Well, let's see now," she said, lying back and ticking them off on the fingers that poked through the bandages.

"There was, *Wanda Finds Waldo*. I wasn't very good in that. Or, how about *Milkmaids on Mars*? I think the Academy made a big mistake not nominating me for an Oscar for that role. I should have at least got Best Supporting Bra. And hey doc, I totally rocked in *Big Band Babette*. You should see what I can do with a trombone."

He felt sick. Felt like he should have known. He looked down and she poked him.

"What's the matter? You didn't catch any of those flicks?"

He shook his head and looked back at her, pleading. It satisfied her. She laughed.

"And you think I've got so much going for me now, do you? You think I can beat this thing and just step back into that great life I had? Well I've got news for you. I can't wait that long. But hey, maybe I can get a new career, huh? At a circus maybe. Or I'm sure there's a market for freak sluts in porn somewhere. I could do like, *Lusty Lepers*, or, or maybe *Tina Takes it Off*, and she can strip off her skin, or, I know, *UV Babes on Broadway*. Whaddya think, Doctor Swan? I could do a fucking calendar, a swimsuit spread in *Psoriasis Illustrated*, why the possibilities are just endless. I can hardly fucking wait! You're right! Why would anyone with my talents and looks want to fucking kill herself?!"

Cynthia slumped back into her pillow and closed her eyes. She was trembling and so was Nathan. He didn't know what to do and Nurse Busybody had poked her head in at least three times during Cynthia's performance.

"Do you want me to leave?" he asked her now.

Eyes still closed, she nodded.

"Yes, thank you Doctor Swan. I'm sure you have patients who actually need you."

He laid his hand on her shoulder. She flinched. He stood up.

"I'll be back tomorrow."

"Whatever."

VII

☞ NATHAN VIEWS A MOVIE, THE CONTENT OF
WHICH LEAVES HIM WITH A RENEWED SENSE
OF DETERMINATION.

Nathan paced the floor of his condo, chainsmoking, drinking. This was not a good scene. He
glanced at his coffee table while he strode back and
forth, saw his newly rented copy of *Big Band
Babette.* There she was. On the cover with her
trombone. He took a deep drag that seared his throat
and kept walking. The VCR was humming, ready,
but Nathan was torn. After seeing Cynthia in the
hospital, he had cancelled the rest of his appointments and gone straight home. For hours he had
lain in bed thinking. He could not get her out of his
mind, he was obsessing and he knew it. At least he
knew it, that was probably a good sign. He almost
wished she had been successful in her attempt. But
the second he thought that, he felt sick. Still did. He
paced and smoked, thinking, and then stopped. It
occurred to him that Cynthia was no longer his
patient. Ergo, he was no longer her doctor. He began

to walk again slowly, thinking it through, and wondering why it should matter anyway. He was certain she was no longer his patient. Certain she would never return for another appointment. He had seen it in her eyes, she was giving up. Why this made him feel better, he did not know. It wasn't just that Cynthia would no longer be his clinical patient, it was something else. What was it? He stooped and butted his smoke, lighting another one immediately. He looked at the video cover again and chewed his lip. An insane idea, but he grabbed onto it. He had stopped thinking of her as a patient and started thinking of her as a woman? Was that it? He wasn't sure, it had been so long. He strode over to his stack of magazines and pulled a different one out, one without Cynthia in it. At least, he hoped. He shook it out, the centrefold flapped down. Nervous, he put his hand on his crotch and rubbed a bit, eyeing the model. Nothing. He flipped through, found a provocative pussy shot. Nothing again. This was madness. He thought he'd been cured. Breaking into a sweat now, he found the original *Playboy*, the one that had started everything. It fell open to Charity's Nazi shot, boots, riding crop, cap. Bingo, baby. We're stirring. No! This can't be! Back to an unfamiliar vixen. Instant shrinkage. Charity again. And we're back in business, folks.

"Damn!" Nathan cried out, tossing both magazines aside.

Being the good doctor that he was, Nathan knew there was one more trial to attend to before he could make a definitive diagnosis. Into the study he headed. Grabbed the medical text and slammed it open on his desk. The freak moved a bit, like a baby waking from sleep and stretching its arms. He knew the rest of the story and slammed the book shut. Okay, so that still worked. He walked back out into the living room and stood there feeling helpless. What had happened to the sense of power he had experienced the other night, when he had fallen to the floor and sobbed? She had given him that. Why now, was he feeling so weak? He marched over to the coffee table and grabbed the video. Slammed it into his VCR before he had time to change his mind. Grabbing a Scotch, he fell into the couch and leaned back to watch.

Sappy music, bad production, and then a naked man with an erection standing in a room. Jeez, they don't waste any time with plot do they, he thought. The naked man was holding his cock and conducting the music with it, wearing a straw boater on his head and a red bow tie. Nathan fast forwarded until he spotted a woman. *Click, whirr, click.* Cynthia. Slightly younger looking, wearing a red wig, but it was her. She was bending over and the conductor was giving her some furious baton action from behind. *And a one, and a two* . . . Nathan cringed inwardly but outwardly his pants were starting to swing. Enough. He clicked it off, he wasn't sure he wanted to see Cynthia's slide action on the trombone. But he did stare at her picture on the video cover while he finished himself off. And he did visualize his own bone sliding in and out of her, making her hit the high notes. And he did, for the very first time ever, look at the freak with a bit of pride. The dude with the bow tie had nothing on Dr. Nathan Swan.

All this was interesting to Nathan, but left him frustrated. He thought about Cynthia lying in the

hospital and knew they would release her tomorrow. He believed she would try to do herself in again.
She was right, of course. From where she lay, the
future probably looked pretty bleak. He'd felt
despair, hopelessness. But he always had patients
who needed him. He believed Cynthia didn't have
anyone. Anyone that is, except him. As a doctor, it
was his duty to save her. And in some bizarre way,
he felt he owed her. She couldn't leave the hospital
and vanish, he had to stop her somehow. With a
sense of purpose, Nathan walked back into his
study, shut the door, and didn't emerge until the
next morning.

VIII

⌒ A MODEST PROPOSAL.

When Nathan arrived the next day, Cynthia was sitting up in bed. She looked pale and exhausted but there was determination in her gaze. He swung into the room with a smile and a bouquet of flowers. She looked at him, suspicious, as he laid them in her lap and settled into a chair.

"Not exactly appropriate, doctor," she said dourly. "Doesn't this violate some doctor-patient thing? Or, if this is your way of trying to convince me not to off myself, it's a waste of money."

But she smelled them and gave a hint of a smile.

Nathan hitched his chair closer and leaned in, conspiratorially.

"I'm not your doctor anymore, for one thing," he began. "Let's face it, if you're not even going to exist after today, I suppose my buying you some farewell flowers isn't going to hurt anyone is it?"

Cynthia blinked. That surprised her.

"I suppose not. Thanks."

"You might as well call me Nathan. After all, I'm

probably the only friend you've got. Right?"

Blunt. Direct. There could be no fucking this up. Nathan had one chance and he was going to take it, but he couldn't mollify her. She was too determined. Cynthia laughed.

"You gonna buy my casket too?"

He took a breath. Here goes, and he better be convincing.

"I will, if you want me to. After you've heard me out."

She rolled her eyes.

"Oh, here we go. I thought we got that over with yesterday."

"We did. I understand. And you're right. There's no cure, the UV doesn't always work, and you're in pretty rough shape. I don't blame you for wanting to give up. I thought about everything you said. You have no one to go home to, no one who gives a shit, and you look like hell and you're in pain. What kind of a life is that? Frankly, now that I know where you're coming from, I'm not surprised you want to pack it in."

Cynthia just looked at him, but he knew he had her interest. She still had enough of an ego to enjoy hearing someone talk about her.

"So, we're on the same page," she said flatly. "So what?"

Nathan nodded, trying to conceal his excitement. Didn't want to get ahead of himself. If he were too eager, she'd sense a trap.

"Listen Cynthia. I have an idea where I can help you and at the same time, you'd be helping me. Hell, you'd be helping medical science for that matter. Just give me a few minutes to explain and if you're not interested, you can tell me to take a hike. Honestly, this just occurred to me last night."

She looked outwardly bored, but her pupils were dilating almost imperceptibly. He at least had her attention.

"I'll have to cut to the chase, spare you a lot of details, but all you need to know is that I've been researching this disease for decades. Nobody knows about this, except for you now, but I've been working on a cure in my spare time."

Cynthia sighed, disbelieving.

"Spare me," she said.

Nathan got angry and his voice got sharper.

"Listen to me!" he demanded.

"I hate to use a tired cliché, but do you know who the fuck I am? I'm one of the top dermatological research specialists in the country. So why not just cut the pity party for a second and listen."

That shut her up. Maybe because he said fuck. Completely out of character. He forged ahead.

"Now listen, here's what I've been thinking. I've got what I believe could be an effective treatment to slow the growth of skin cells. I'm not entirely sure about this, but I need to test it out. I'll warn you this is not FDA approved, but if it works it will be a major breakthrough. I'm more excited about this than you can imagine, even though I may not look like it. I don't show excitement well, I'm sorry."

Cynthia sat up straighter, it was his tone of secrecy that had really grabbed her. This was kind of neat.

"So, let me get this straight," she said. "You want me to be your guinea pig? Is that it?"

He nodded.

"Yes, don't you see? It would help us both out. But I've also got some conditions that might just help you decide one way or the other. Do you want to hear more?"

Cynthia nodded slowly. "Okay, sure doc."

"This treatment, it's a combination of several things. It's not just a cream, UV rays, oral medication, or steroid injections. It's more of a, how shall I put it, lifestyle modification, biofeedback, um, a bunch of stuff. More like you being an alcoholic and going to rehab for treatment. You get detoxed, then you get counselling and workshops, and a rapid vigorous lifestyle change. Is any of this making sense?"

"Maybe," Cynthia said. "What all's involved?"

Nathan grinned finally, and took a deep breath. Maybe this would work.

"Okay, you would have to commit to about three months, maybe six, I'm not sure. A lot of this treatment is alternative. I've developed ointments from herbs, teas, tonics, and tapes for you to listen to. Natural sunshine will be a major factor, and relaxation techniques and hypnosis will also be part of the package."

"Hypnosis? Are you going to make me bark like a dog?"

He laughed, and relaxed.

"Not unless you want me to. So Cynthia, tell me, would you be willing to give this a shot? For both of us?"

She stared at the ceiling, struggling within herself. Nathan could tell she wanted to believe him, still wanted to believe something would work. She turned her head to look at him.

"Where's the clinic? And look, I don't want to sit

around with a bunch of losers having group therapy or anything. Could I get private treatment?"

She frowned.

"And who's going to pay for this?"

Here comes the difficult part. She'd either love it or hate it.

"That's the best part," he said. "Because I don't want anyone else to know about this project, I want to do it at my home. You would have your own room, I would teach you how to cook the healing meals, and aside from our sessions, you could come and go as you please with as much or as little privacy as you wish. I realize it's unorthodox, but drastic times call for drastic measures as they say, and I'd say your suicide attempt was as drastic as it comes.

"As to my end of things, I've been wanting to test this for a while now, but had no idea how to find a subject, patient, who would be willing to go this route."

Nathan didn't add, *and someone who can keep her mouth shut*, and didn't mention that he knew about her eviction.

"It would not cost you a dime, you'd be doing me a favour, really."

That seemed to cinch it. Cynthia actually sniffled.

"Are you sure you want some low-budget porn queen in your house? Wouldn't that be bad for your reputation?"

Nathan handed her a Kleenex.

"Look, if it makes you feel any better, I went out last night and rented *Big Band Babette*. Now there are no secrets. And by the way, I thought you deserved an Oscar."

That, at least, got a laugh.

"Wow, you're a piece of work, doc. Fuck, what have I got to lose? "

"Does this mean you'll do it?" he asked. "I have to know now, because I'll book off my clinic."

"Sure, why the hell not."

Nathan stood up, he was shaking.

"Okay, go home, pack up some things and if you can keep it together until next Monday, we'll give this thing a shot. Deal?"

He stuck out his hand.

"Deal," she said, and shook it, wincing.

Nathan left the hospital room a happy man. He got in his car, turned the key, and thought a minute. Okay, now just one thing left to do. Make up some kind of cure.

IX

☞ A PLAYFUL MOMENT FOR NATHAN, A RARE
OCCURRENCE BUT ONE IN WHICH HE
REVELS WITH ABANDON.

It was the day before Cynthia was due to arrive.
Nathan was on his hands and knees scrubbing
the kitchen floor, whistling. He had spent the last
few days fixing up the condo, even repainting the
spare room, Cynthia's room, blue. Like her eyes.
Gone out and bought new sheets, a duvet, fluffy
feather pillows, and a Monet. Cleaned out the record
store, having no idea of her musical tastes. Well,
aside from big band, that is. *Pa-dum-pum.* And his
cupboards and fridge were both crammed with
everything from sinful delicacies to health food.
Today, all his windows were open and a rare sunny
day flooded the spacious rooms. It was an omen, he
was sure of it. In between polishing and shopping
and scouring, he had even found time to invent a
cure for psoriasis. He was mad. A mad scientist.
Johnny's in the basement, mixin' up the medicine . . . .
He had never entertained a woman in this suite

before, ever. Oops! He grinned like a schoolboy
caught lying. Not entertained, Nathan. Treated. He
had never treated a woman in this suite before, ever.
Ah, life was good. He lay on his back on the clean
cool tiles, spread his legs wide and whipped the big
guy out. Just for the hell of it. Why the fuck not? We
all might as well enjoy this sunshine. He laughed
out loud. It's part of the "treatment" after all, isn't
it? Nuthin' wrong with old sol. He played with himself a bit, idly flipping the serpent back and forth,
enjoying the feel of it smacking his inner thighs.
Enjoying the sound of it. Just like Adam and Eve and
the snake, all three of them would be so cozy here.
He hooted with laughter. Only difference was,
Cynthia would be like the snake. What a fucking
riot. This was too much. Too much fun, settle down
Mr. Big Scientist Man. Just 'cause you went and
cured psoriasis doesn't mean you can get all sloppy
now. You still have an image to maintain. And
speaking of image, pulling on longfellow now,
what's up with these porn dudes? After watching *Big
Band Babette*, Nathan had gone out and rented a
month's worth of porno videos and watched them
all within a few days. Part of the research, a tax
write-off. He needed to get familiar with technique.
Well you know, just in case. Not one tape had made
him hard, but he took descriptive notes. Then he
would put on something from the Charity Heatherton
collection and mimic all the male porn stars' moves
in his head, beating off to her moans and sighs. She
was definitely a pro, he thought, now that he had
viewed the entire library. But none of those guys did
her justice. He looked down his chest at the freak as
he lay there on the floor. It was standing proud and

strong, casting a shadow on the tiles. He looked at the shadow. Hmmm. Two o'clock. And shrieked with uncontrollable laughter. Pumping himself again luxuriously, almost purring in the sunlight, Nathan visualized Charity. Cynthia. Now it seemed she was the only thing he thought about. She needed some dialogue. Maybe he could write a decent script. They could rehearse it together, he was dying to try out his new-found knowledge. His hand stopped for a second. Hey, he had a video camera in the bed-room. After he cured her, maybe he could help her get back into the business. The possibilities were endless and fascinating. Nathan couldn't remember the last time he had an *incident*. A month ago? Two? How could he have lived like that for this long? But things were different now. Yeah, things were definitely *looking up*. Nathan was hesitant to analyze the situation too much, didn't want to jinx it. Yet . . .

DIFFERENTIAL DIAGNOSES: Possibility for break-through in psoriasis study? *Partly*. Insanity? *Probably*. Falling in love? *Nah, couldn't be.*

Yet . . .

He groaned now, thinking about Cynthia made his balls feel like exploding. As much as he loved her peeling skin and its shiny, rough texture, he was safe in the knowledge that even if he cured her – when he cured her that is – he had happily discovered he could get aroused by her in her natural state. Either way. Seemingly impossible, but true. Clear liquid droplets were forming on the head of the freak now, *faster, Science Boy, faster*. He closed his eyes and pictured Cynthia naked, red, scaly, and bending over to put a roast in his oven. He shot like a rocket into the sun, and the shadow time rolled quickly backwards into nothing. He would have to wash the floor again.

X

☞ REVELATION OF AN UGLY TRUTH PROMPTED BY
AN URGENT COMPULSION ON NATHAN'S PART.

Midnight. Nathan was restless. Everything was in readiness for Cynthia's arrival and he didn't know what to do next. He thought he had everything figured out, but now that he had time to think, he wondered. Was he really as together as he thought? Maybe he was deluding himself, thinking he had a grip. Certainly wouldn't be the first time. Maybe, maybe. He felt some crucial piece of evidence supporting his newfound optimism was missing. Nathan walked to his balcony and stood outside in the darkness, looking east to the lights of downtown. He felt apprehensive, and the freak, always a reliable barometer of his inner turmoil, was acting up. But this time it was like a cranky child. Like a kid demanding attention, but not sure what he really wants. Nathan listened to the taxis honking below, and rubbed himself against the railing. Nothing. He didn't feel his usual compulsion to race back into the study and relieve himself, this was different. Not a pressing need, more an aching, like unfinished business. But what? He frowned, thinking. Earlier, he had been so excited about Cynthia's impending visit, so sure of himself. Now, he felt doubt. A cabbie laid on his horn, and Nathan yelled at him. *Shut the fuck up!* But it gave him an idea. He had been staring at it the whole time. Downtown. He needed to make another trip to skid row. A final test, see if he could still get it up for a hooker. See if he still needed them. Now that he thought of it, he couldn't wait, didn't even care what the outcome was. And he had to do it before Cynthia showed up, had to know. He raced back into his apartment, grabbed his keys, and headed down to his car. No time to rent one, he'd take the chance he wouldn't be recognized. As he settled into the car and lit a cigarette, pulling out into traffic, he felt much better. This felt right, it was the missing link, he was sure of it. Even the freak seemed content.

Nathan drove like a maniac until he hit East Hastings, where traffic slowed. He opened his window and leaned out, wondering why there was so much activity on a Wednesday night. Then it dawned on him. *Fuck.* It was the last Wednesday of the month, Welfare Wednesday, Mardi Gras, Rodeo Days. The worst night of the month to be down here. The one night everyone had money. Money they would spend all in this one evening, availing themselves of what the street had to offer. Dealers would be out in full force, and hookers and cops. Nathan hit his steering wheel with his hand. Not a good night to be cruising, not a good night to be here at all. Traffic was now stopped for some reason. Could be anything, someone lying in the middle of the street, a take-down, smashed bottles, anything. He sat there, watching the carnival, knowing the hooker thing was out of the question. Too many cops, for starters. His car inched towards the Balmoral Hotel. Something was happening right in front, in the doorway. A small crowd was gathering and a girl was screaming. Nathan looked to see what was going on, but a small crowd and a girl screeching just wasn't all that unusual down here. Until he heard her screaming the one word that would get his attention – *Doctor*.

Oh, this night just keeps getting better.

His first reaction was to slink down in his seat, until he realized how ridiculous that was. As if anyone would know. Her shrill voice was cutting into his brain, *Get a doctor! Somebody help me, I need a doctor over here!*

Nathan cursed. He looked around. Christ, where was a doctor when you need one. They should have fuckin' doctors patrolling this area along with the cops, he thought. But it was impossible to ignore the shrieking. No one else probably even heard her, what with all the other commotion, but it sliced into Nathan's head. He pulled over, and put his car in park. Didn't know what he would be able to do without a medical bag, not to mention this wasn't his specialty. Fat chance the victim would be lying on the pavement with a bad case of dermatitis. Still. He walked over to the few people still hanging around. The girl was freaking, crying, screaming, alternately standing up waving her arms around and bending down over some guy sprawled on the sidewalk. Nathan elbowed a couple of drunken bystanders out of the way. *I'm a doctor. Let me through.* They stumbled back a couple steps, glaring at him. Nathan knelt down beside the motionless young man. Crying chick was incomprehensible. *He just fell down, I don't know, he's my boyfriend, can you help him, I didn't know, maybe he did too much, I don't know, I wasn't watching, make him wake up . . .*

Nathan picked up a thin arm and noticed a fresh track mark as he felt for a pulse. That didn't surprise him. He moved the kid's long hair off his face and turned his head, to feel his carotid pulse. That did surprise him. He gasped and fell back on his heels. Then he fell right over as a big cop pushed his way through, followed by an ambulance crew. Barking orders, *out of the way*, the cop shoving people back as the paramedics hunkered down. Nathan crawled off to the side, feeling sick. Picked himself up slowly, shaking, feeling as one with the rest of the passers-by, dishevelled, unfocused, mean. He stood for a minute, collecting his thoughts, staring at the wall beside the Balmoral's front door. There was a poster in front of his face. After a minute of heavy breathing and staring, it swam into focus. *Appearing tonight at the Balmoral. Bobby Brightman and the Barn Animals.*

Nathan swore. The thought of a junkie hooker right now made him want to vomit. He headed to his car and did not look back. Experiment over.

XI

~ THE ARRIVAL.

Nathan was sitting perched on the edge of his couch when the buzzer sounded. His knee jerked and knocked over a glass of white wine. *Shit.* Leaving the wine soaking into the carpet, he jumped up to buzz Cynthia in. He thought a welcoming glass of wine was appropriate. Hoped it was. He knew she had drunk an entire bottle of the stuff when she tried to kill herself, hoped she didn't have bad memories of white wine. But if she did, he had an entire bar stock to choose from. Just thought it would be nice to have it all poured and cold and, *knock knock*, there she is. His hands were shaking, he was so nervous.

Never thought he'd be this lame. Moved to the door, wiping his sweaty palms on his jeans. Opened it, and waved her in with a deep bow.

"Just set your bags down anywhere Cynthia," he said, moving back to the couch trying to look casual and unruffled. He sat down and took a sip of wine.

She stood there in the doorway for a few minutes, wrapped in her hat and glasses, scarf and shapeless baggy clothing. All she had was one small suitcase. She set it down and took off her sunglasses. Gave him a tiny, shy smile. His heart braked. She looked so vulnerable and yet so bulky. He rose again.

"Can I take your coat, and hat?" he asked politely, walking over to her.

Cynthia took a step back, seemed jumpy, like she was the first day in his office. How long ago was that now, he wondered. She took off her hat, her long hair falling down her back. He helped her off with her coat and hung it and the hat in the hallway closet. Picked up her bag, and motioned her inside. Cynthia walked lightly, her feet still sore, reminding Nathan she was here for help. God help me, he thought. He sat back down and watched her walk around, peering at the artwork, running a cracked hand lightly on the sculptures, looking up and down, examining her new home.

"Would you like a glass of wine?" he asked, holding the bottle up.

"White wine?"

He grimaced and put the bottle down. Fool.

"Sorry, I guess you've had enough white wine to last a lifetime," he said, wincing at his choice of words. *Can't do anything right.* But she gave him a sweet smile anyway.

"How about a glass of red wine?" he burbled. "Or anything, for that matter. If you want it, I probably have it."

"All part of the ground-breaking treatment?" she asked, revealing some of her earlier spunk.

He blushed. *Blushed.* Can you imagine.What happened to Nathan Swan Porn King, the other day? Where did he go?

"I'm sorry," he mumbled. "No, I just thought you might want to relax and settle in. We won't start treatment until tomorrow."

Cynthia nodded, trying to open the heavy glass door to the balcony. He leaped up to help her and standing beside her like that, he could smell her hair. She had washed it and it smelled like fruit. She looked up at him gratefully when he threw back the door. Yes, wasn't he just a superhero now. I can open doors with a single shove. And act like an asshole with a single word. I'm fuckin' amazing, folks. As Cynthia stepped onto the balcony, she turned to Nathan.

"I'll have a martini, if you can manage it. Vodka, dry, with a twist."

Well, don't make it too easy, he thought.

"Coming right up."

In the kitchen, shaking it up, the ice rattling so loud it hurt his ears, he strained around the corner to look for her. She was standing on the balcony, her back to him, hair lifting slightly in the breeze. All the blonde was gone and there she stood. The brown-haired woman of his dreams. On his balcony, on his terms, and maybe one night on his big prick. *What? Did I think that?* He shook his head. What was wrong with him, lately anyhow. He poured the ice cold booze into a martini glass and wiping his hands on a dishtowel, returned to the living room and stepped out onto the balcony with her.

"Here you go."

She took the glass without looking at him, staring at the mountains.

"It's beautiful here," she sighed, face to the sun.

Although it was a corny thought, he thought it anyway – so are you. So are you the way the sunlight reflects off the hints of red in your hair, the silvery plate-like plaques on your neck. You are a goddess. Guess that makes me a god. Doctor. God. Same thing. All these thoughts sped through Nathan's mind as he stood on the balcony sipping his wine. After a few minutes of silence, Cynthia spoke.

"I guess I'm getting treatment in a way now, anyways," she said, eyes closed, head back. "I mean, I'm getting some sun."

Nathan rested an elbow on the balcony railing and turned sideways to look at her. What the fuck was he going to do with her? He had spent hours working out formulas and, to be fair, he actually had done a lot of research on psoriasis and alternative medicines. But he was afraid most of it would be a crock. He had simply gone mad, that was all there was to it. He was as mad as Terence Stamp in *The Collector*. The weirdo who kept that woman captive in his basement, trying to make her love him. The guy who collected dead butterflies. Nathan shuddered a bit. No, he wasn't like that. He couldn't be. Unlike Terence Stamp, who ended up killing the girl, Nathan was saving the girl. Didn't matter if his cure was a pile of shit. If it wasn't for him, she'd be dead right now. Yesiree. And come to think of it, so would he probably. Dead inside. He felt his heart surge, and that wasn't all.

"So, how's this experiment going to work, Nathan?" Cynthia asked now, looking at him. "The treatments, I mean. How will we start?"

Nathan put on his doctor face and turned forward, speaking in the general direction of the ocean. He found it difficult to speak directly to Cynthia when he was laying it on.

"Well," he coughed and cleared his throat. "There are a number of things we're going to try. You remember this might take months?"

She nodded, taking another sip.

"Although, as you know, there is no known cause for psoriasis, I believe there is some link to our immune system. Genetics could play a part, but you don't have any family history that you know of. And as I think I told you during your office visits, there is some school of thought that links it to stress. So, genetics aside, I'm concentrating on the other perceived causes and triggers. We're going to deal with all of it. I've made up some detoxifying herbal teas, and I have a supply of shark liver oil which is extremely rich in alkylglycerols, or AKGs, compounds known to stimulate the body's immune system."

"Shark liver oil?" she asked, shivering a bit.

"Well, think about it," Nathan said, warming to his subject. "Sharks live to be over one hundred years old. They have an incredible resistance to infections and tumours and AKGs are a source of immunity. The AKGs are found in the liver oil of deep water sharks, most particularly the Greenland Shark. It's a natural supplement in the liver oil, nothing weird or freaky."

Cynthia pitched her head to one side, quizzically.

"So, what did you do, go out and harpoon a shark just for me?"

She laughed, but Nathan could tell she was impressed. Whew! Shit, it sounded plausible even to him. Amazing what you can crib off the net these days. He stood up a little straighter. Maybe he could pull this off after all and besides, he did have shark liver oil and it was good for the immune system. He wasn't a total charlatan. A trial of cyclosporine was also in the cards, but that was so medicinal, he figured she would rather hear about the alternative therapies first.

"Have you been bathing regularly, or do you find the water hurts your skin?" he asked.

Cynthia shrugged.

"It depends. Sometimes it's just too painful. I definitely can't have any perfumed oils or bath salts, but sometimes I want to soak in baby oil or something to loosen everything up and make it softer."

Nathan took a drink.

"Well, I've got some Dead Sea salts, and I'm going to want you to soak in them too. They'll pull the toxins from your body. Three baths per week for at least a month."

"Dead Sea salts? Are they really from the Dead Sea?"

"Yes, Cynthia. Yes, they really are."

A breeze came up and blew Cynthia's hair around her tanned face. It was an eerie breeze, carrying a bit of a chill and the sky seemed to shift with it, like cards shuffling into place.

"I've been to the Dead Sea, you know," she said to Nathan.

"Really? Have you?"

"No."

XII

A few weeks passed and things were settling into somewhat of a comfortable routine. Cynthia had learned how to prepare all her blenderized health shakes. They were going for long walks when the sun shone and she wore Nathan's special ointment on her face to attract the correct rays. He taught her breathing exercises, let her indulge in music therapy over the headphones, got her dipping into Emu oil and soaking in the Dead Sea salts. For the first week, she had pretty much stayed in her room except for the walks and to eat. Now, they were managing to enjoy some plain old quality time together some evenings by the fire. Her psoriasis wasn't getting any better, but then again it wasn't getting any worse either. The lotions he prepared had actually made the pain more bearable and she wasn't cracking open as much as she used to. She was grateful for that and made him dinner one night. While she was bustling around in the kitchen as quickly as her tender hands would allow, Nathan sat in the living room with a Scotch watching her. From his point of view, things couldn't have been going much better. He couldn't even remember what life had been like alone. The sounds of her chopping vegetables, running water, opening the fridge, the tiniest most insignificant sounds made his heart swell. At night, he slept soundly, comforted in the fact she was breathing in another room. He was pleased she was coming around emotionally. Her spirits seemed better, he thought he could hear her humming in the kitchen now. She was beginning to trust him and trust herself again. And that was a good thing. But inevitably, with everything good in Nathan Swan's life, something bad must follow. And just when Cynthia was relaxing and growing into her new home, he was starting to feel suffocated. Not because she was crowding him in terms of personal space, but she was crowding his brain. He had been so uptight in the beginning, worried she might leave, he hadn't thought much about his problem, his primordial urges. Hadn't had any. But now, every time he looked at her, he felt the familiar constriction building. He was beginning to have fantasies and not about winning a Nobel Prize for the all-holy psoriasis cure. Nope, Nathan Swan was having your typical garden variety fuck fantasies. Even now, as she stood on a stool to reach a top cupboard, he looked at the backs of her legs with the roughened skin, patches all shiny with ointment, and could feel an impending erection. He clenched his jaw and took another drink. It was becoming increasingly difficult to control himself and sooner or later she would spot the telltale bulge. He'd been thinking about this for awhile and last night had told her he would like to take photographs of her naked. Of course, he said it in a completely detached clinical manner, explaining it would be helpful to document her psoriasis on film. She had merely shrugged her shoulders.

"That makes sense. It's not like I'm not used to taking my clothes off in front of men. And hey, you're a doctor, it's not like you haven't seen naked women before. Sure, what the hell."

And she had gone back to eating her pasta.

While he, on the other hand, had to get up and leave the room to beat the big guy back down. How easy was that? He was quivering all over. Sometimes he was convinced he was a genius, convinced. Maybe he should re-jig his fantasy and receive the Nobel Prize after all. But only after he had put in a prize winning performance with the psoriasis poster girl.

"Are we having wine with dinner?" she asked from the kitchen.

He wrenched himself away from giving his acceptance speech.

"Sure, why not? Don't forget we're doing the big photo shoot after dinner, though."

Cynthia giggled at that and walked out to let him struggle with the corkscrew.

"Here you go, Rigby, you big stud," she said, handing it over and wiggling seductively back to the kitchen.

"Rigby?" he yelled to her back. "Who's Rigby?"

"Nothing, never mind. Old news."

Rigby. What kind of a fucking name is that, he thought, yarding on the corkscrew. Some guy she did in a movie probably. A satisfying pop of the cork, and Nathan poured a couple glasses of red wine. Served up nice and robust with a healthy slice of jealousy. The big guy shifted. Nathan glanced down and thought, Rigby, huh? I'll show you Rigby.

He swallowed a gulp of wine, spilling a bit down his chin and wiped it with the back of his hand. He could not let things get out of control, not now. Not ever. The photos were just the ticket to keep things in perspective. To keep him honest. They would tide him over nicely, he believed. Now if only he could keep *Rigby* under wraps until he shot off a roll of Polaroids. Then he could retreat to his room and settle in with them. He was fine with photos. Had been dealing with photographs for years, they would keep his unrealistic urges at bay. He looked up as Cynthia called for dinner. She had made a wonderful meal, he had no idea she could cook so well, and Nathan knew he wouldn't taste a single mouthful.

XIII

☞ Cᴠɴᴛʜɪᴀ's ᴅɪsᴄᴏᴠᴇʀʏ.

They were standing in his office, a little tipsy from all the wine and Nathan was turning on the bright lights for the photo session. Cynthia was sitting on a chair in her robe, making funny comments, and giggling as he tried to set up some semblance of clinical lighting. He looked so serious, she thought, what's the big deal? It's only a Polaroid for Christ's sake. In fact, he almost looked kind of cute, tripping over lamp cords, dropping the camera, his glasses sliding down his nose. Maybe it was the wine, but Cynthia was feeling the most comfortable in her skin that she'd felt in months. If it wasn't for the pain and itching, at times she could forget she even had psoriasis. Nathan didn't flinch when he touched her, didn't look at her strangely, and they had both examined her skin so closely together in the past few weeks, she was becoming used to it.

Not happy with it, just more used to it. She figured she had been in denial before, that's why she went into shock each time she saw herself. But, Nathan's cure was going to work. She was sure of it. Her skin was feeling softer, more pliable and not as angry looking as before. Nathan was so smart, and so kind, how could this not work. And even if it took months, she didn't care if he didn't. She looked around. What a cool pad. She could live with it for months. And now that she was used to the regimen, she could even relax and have a bit of fun. Like tonight, watching Nathan trying to be all professional when she knew he didn't have a clue about photography. Oh well, she sure as hell wasn't looking like Cindy Crawford now, was she? The thought made her giggle which caused Nathan to look up from the floor where he was plugging in yet another light.

"What's so funny?"

"Nothing," she said, stifling a laugh. "Well, that's not true. I was just thinking what a useless pair we are. You're supposed to be a photographer and you'll probably wind up electrocuting yourself and I'm supposed to be a model and I look like Swamp Thing. This just struck me as so totally pathetic, I had to laugh."

And she did. The first really good laugh he'd heard from her. It lit up her face even though it split open a few cracks. Then he started. She was rocking back and forth now, holding her stomach, her robe falling open and her breasts showing. It was infectious. Nathan started to grin, then chuckle, and then, trying to stand up and tripping over yet another cord, he fell flat on his ass, which caused her to squeal even louder and him to give up and lie there, helpless, shaking with mirth and feeling hopelessly crazy. It was the most fun either of them had experienced in ages. They were both so used to putting themselves down, criticizing themselves overly harshly, and denying themselves a silly moment, that nothing could have amused them more than actually taking a moment to laugh at themselves. It was wild relief and when the fit was over, Nathan was grateful. It had taken the edge off and he was feeling much more sure of keeping himself in check when Cynthia disrobed for the camera. Which she did immediately and quickly. In one fluid motion, she stood up tall and flung the robe dramatically onto a chair.

"Well, here I am Mr. Swan. Have your way with me."

Thank God for the camera. Nathan grabbed it and held it up to his face to hide any signs of impending embarrassment on his part. At first, Cynthia fooled around, posing haughtily, nose turned up, striking a regal pose and a running commentary.

"And now ladies and gentlemen, our model will feature this year's fall collection of dead skin. You will note the seasonal orange colour, lightly dotted with specks of glittery silver flakes. Lovely for evening wear, perfect for a night at the opera."

Click. Click.

After a couple of high fashion runway poses, Cynthia switched from haughty to naughty. Nathan could hardly contain his pants and bent over at the waist to hide his rising emotion. Cynthia didn't do anything too risqué, no spread shots or anything quite so vulgar, but she managed to be sexy and coy at the same time. Nathan's head was beading with sweat. From all the lights, no doubt. Finally, he had to tell her to stop.

"Okay Cynthia, now we need some real close-up shots of the lesions. This is a scientific photo shoot, after all."

She pouted prettily but stood still and followed his directions. Arm out. Hold it. *Click.* Palms up. Steady now. *Click.* Close-up of the navel ring, the feet, the neck, the shoulders. *Click. Click. Click. Click.*

Finished. The roll was shot and photos of Cynthia were lying all over the study in various stages of development. She put her robe back on, so nonchalantly, so matter of factly, and picked up a photo. Nathan watched for her reaction. Scrutinizing it closely, she sniffed a bit, and then laid it back down. She was getting used to her looks, and he couldn't have been more pleased.

"That was fun!" she said, and leaned over to give him a peck on the cheek.

"I'm tired. I think I'll crash now,"

Gathering up the photos, he nodded.

"Okay see you in the morning, then."

Watching her disappear down the hall, he listened for her door to close, and collapsed against a wall. He ached all over from trying to hold everything in while she had pranced and posed and glittered and oozed under the bright, hot lights. Was it possible she was getting better? He shook his head vigorously. Good thing he took the photos. It might be worth documenting something other than his desires. Quickly, as if he was doing something illegal, he scooped up the photos and retreated to his bedroom, clutching them to his chest like a newborn baby.

He turned off the overhead light, and lit a couple of bedside lamps with rose shades. They cast a seductive glow onto the white chenille bedspread where Nathan lay out his booty. Possessively, he kissed each one before he laid it on the bed. The clinical shots, the ones of lesion close-ups, he stacked in a neat pile off to the side. But the poses he arranged in a semi-circle. He couldn't believe his luck when Cynthia had decided to act up and be foolish. Couldn't have asked for better jerk-off photos. Although he still could have had a mighty fine time with the close-ups, had been doing that for years, now he had real peeler poses. He could hardly wait, couldn't get his pants off fast enough. Standing at the side of the bed, he couldn't help but feel blessed. The freak was doing semi-circles of its own accord, like a divining rod, swinging from one photo to the next, until he took himself in hand. She was so precious in that one. Peeking over her sad arm, bright eyes, dimples. Ahhh. He stroked himself with exquisitely firm slowness for that one. And the next one, he grinned at it. She was such a vixen. Quicker now. He had never felt so huge. Never felt so loving of himself. His breath was ragged, it wasn't going to take long this time. Didn't matter, he had the pictures. Could examine them at his leisure later. Just enjoy it. Just remember to. Breathe. Bites his lip! There's blood in his mouth and it sets him off big time. Exploding, imploding, his knees buckle, he gasps noisily, falls towards the bed and catches himself with one arm outstretched. His penis rests on a photo, dribbling bits of semen onto her face. Nathan has never felt so full and so drained at the same time. His heart pounds irregularly and his gasping begins to slow.

But Cynthia's has only started. Hand over her

mouth, eyes popping from her head, and trying desperately not to make a sound, she is bent over and scurrying as fast as her wrapped-up feet will allow. Back to her bedroom. Oh. My. God. Oh. My God. It's all she can think, her head is swimming and she, *please God*, just wants to get into her room without Nathan knowing she had seen everything. And when we say everything, ladies and gentlemen of the jury, we mean everything. Every gol darn inch of that puppy. Swear in the witness, please.

Now, Miss Poole, do you swear that the testimony you are about to give in this case is the truth, the whole truth, and nothing but the truth?

I do. But you're never going to believe it.

Is it your testimony today, that the defendant was carrying a loaded weapon when last you saw him?

It is, but I've never seen anything like it!

Can you describe the weapon for the jury, Miss Poole.

I, um, I don't think so. Can I stand up and show the jury with my hands, how big it was?

Yes, you can do that.

[Courtroom is hushed]

Let the record show that Miss Poole is holding her hands apart approximately . . . no that's not possible. I cite you for contempt, Miss Poole! Take her away! Order in the court! Take her away! She's insane!

[Female jurors are dropping like flies, fainting, while the witness is led away screaming]

No! No! It's true! You have to believe me! I saw it! I did! I'm not crazy!

Cynthia reaches her room finally, and closes the door quietly. She sits on her bed, heart skittering, and turns off the lights. In the dark, she sits and replays the scene over and over. When she had impulsively done her performance for the photo shoot, she had wondered if Nathan might use the pictures for his own pleasure. She'd been around enough horny men in her day to be able to spot the signs. In fact, she had found it most endearing watching him in the last few days trying to hide his growing attraction. And when she was cooking dinner for him earlier, she had felt happy and normal for the first time in a long time. Maybe, ever. It was hard to believe someone could find her attractive again. In her state. But it wasn't until she had witnessed the spectacle in his bedroom, that she knew for sure. She understood then. He actually got off on the mess her skin was in. It turned him on. How about that? Having done porn for years, Cynthia was used to freaks. Men got off on the weirdest things, so why not Nathan. She remembered her initial appointments with him in his office, when she still looked relatively good with just a few patches of disruption. She had picked up on a sense of loathing at that time. Erroneously, she had attributed that distaste to her ugly bits. But now, upon reflection, she realized it wasn't that at all. And when he was jerking off to her photos, she had sensed something else. It wasn't just lust. She had seen tears in his eyes, and her heart had done a flip. She saw the way he had lovingly laid out her photos, reverentially, with care. There was more going on with Nathan than some kinky sexual trip. It touched her. Now, she touched herself. And while she pleasured herself, she pictured his face. And more. Yes, ladies and gentleman of the jury, much, much more.

XIV

A FINAL EXPERIMENT.

The next day, Cynthia and Nathan greeted each other as usual, over a healthy breakfast. The photo shoot of the night before was not mentioned by either one of them. Nathan was thinking Cynthia looked much better today, more relaxed, more desirable than ever. Is it possible the cure was working? He examined her skin after they had eaten, but the proximity to her was unnerving. She was electric, and he had to excuse himself from her company several times throughout their sessions. Cynthia was watching him closely now. Every time he had to leave the room, she watched him go with a sense of yearning. When he touched her skin, so gently, so calmly, her heart lurched. She wanted him to touch her breast, her lips. And she knew he wanted to, but he was too professional, too shy, or too afraid. The entire day flew by, with both of them carrying their secret, both of them struggling. That evening, while they were sitting by the fire, Nathan made mention of a new treatment he wanted to try.

It was time, he said, for Cynthia to bark like a dog.

"Hypnosis?" she asked.

Nathan nodded, but couldn't bring himself to look her in the eyes.

"Yes, I think maybe we can convince those determined skin cells of yours to stop their incessant multiplying. It's worth a shot, anyway. Are you up for it?"

Maybe it was the way he said it, or maybe it was just Cynthia's heightened awareness of all things Nathan, but she knew something was up. Something other than simple hypnosis. It excited her but she remained calm and agreed to try it.

"Well, no time like the present," he said, and she noticed him trembling.

"What do you want me to do?" she asked.

Cynthia would have done anything for him. But whereas before she would have tried anything to rid herself of the skin disease, now she wasn't as eager to lose it. Nathan liked it. It turned him on. And that turned her on. He took off his glasses and gave them a quick wipe with his sleeve. He did have nice eyes. Blue, like hers. He cleared his throat.

"Well, first I think we should have a drink of brandy. Just something to relax you, make you more amenable to suggestion," he said.

Cynthia nodded, but was suspicious. She watched him get up to mix the drinks.

"I'll just be a minute," he called from the kitchen.

Once again, Cynthia was ahead of him. Or rather, behind him. She stood in the doorway, peeking around the corner and saw him pour some kind of powder into one of the glasses of brandy. She didn't know what it was, but she'd been around. Probably some kind of date rape drug. Charming, she thought, and tiptoed back to the living room. Nathan returned with the brandy, and set the glasses down with a clatter. He was uptight but Cynthia was serene. She picked up her glass and took a sip but didn't swallow. He eyed her warily. She stood up then, still clutching her glass and started walking to the kitchen.

"Where are you going?" he asked.

"I'm just going to get some candles. I think that would help me relax too, don't you?"

Nathan grunted in assent, thinking he should have thought of that. While in the kitchen, Cynthia poured the tainted drink in the sink and filled her glass again with brandy. Grabbing a couple of candles, she returned. It was time for an Oscar winning performance and she was up for it. She even had butterflies, stagefright, it was delicious. Nathan's face looked drawn in the candlelight and she knew he was having some kind of inner struggle. He looked pained every time she took a sip of brandy. After about ten minutes, Cynthia let her eyelids drop ever so slightly and ran a feeble hand across her brow. She sprawled into the couch.

"You're right, Nathan. This brandy is making me feel really relaxed. Is it hot in here, or is it just me?"

Nathan looked worried but perversely determined. She stretched further into the couch and smiled at him with a half-lidded look of contentment.

"Jeez, I think I must be tired or something. Maybe we should start the hypnosis now, what do you think?"

Nathan nodded, sweat building up on his brow.

"Good idea, just lie back and relax, maybe take one more drink and then lie down. I'm just going to talk to you. There's no gold watch swinging around or anything. Just listen to my voice."

Cynthia was having a great time. She struggled to sit up and took a huge belt of brandy, some of it missing her mouth and spilling down the front of her blouse.

"Ooops! Sorry!" she said, giggling and trying unsuccessfully to wipe her front.

Her elbow slipped off the couch, all planned, and her head and shoulders slumped over the edge. She lay still. Nathan sat there looking at her, vibrating in his chair with pent-up anxiety and anticipation. She moved slightly and he could barely hear her muffled voice.

"Cynthia?" he asked, leaning over and touching her hair. "Cynthia, can you hear me?"

Her head raised up about an inch and fell back down, hair trailing on the carpet.

"Arf," she said. "Arf, arf."

And was silent.

Nathan waited a full minute before he moved from his chair. He had never done anything like this before. Although he was terrified and even shocked at his own behaviour, nothing would have prevented him from doing this. Something had compelled him, some urgency, some part of his own sickness or madness. If this was a spell, it was the worst and best one he had ever experienced. Downing the last of his own brandy, he moved. Grabbing Cynthia's limp body in his arms he carried her into his bedroom. He felt disgusted with himself but the freak was pounding inside his pants. Gently, he laid her on the bed and arranged her hair so it fanned out across the pillows. He took a moment and looked at

her lying there, like an angel. Then he scrambled
with his belt, his shirt, his underwear that was practically being ripped at the seams by the freak.
Finally, he was naked and the big guy was looking
all regal, a deep royal purple, a glistening crown on
its head. It was pointed right at her, like it was a
compass and she was due north. Nathan had lost his
mind, he was sure of it. Walking over to the bed he
looked down at her again and groaned with pain
and desire and a longing he had never before experienced. Her long legs were slightly parted, tanned
in some places, peeling and scaly in others. He
leaned over, breathing heavily, and touched the
hem of her skirt. Slowly, ever so slowly, he began to
pull it up. She moaned slightly. He stopped, cringing,
and stared anxiously at her face. Silence again. He
wet his lips and clambered onto the bed, kneeling.
Spread her legs and positioned himself in between
on his knees, looking up at her face every few seconds to check. His heart felt like it would explode out
of his chest. Again, he daintily lifted the hem of her
skirt and pulled it up towards her tiny waist ever so
slowly. With each new inch of skin he discovered, he
seemed to grow an inch if that were possible. His
penis was so huge it was practically nudging her
private parts even from his position down by her
knees. He saw her panties now. White cotton panties,
all smooth and clean, like virginal velvet. He gulped.
Pulled the skirt even higher, to her waist and then
above. The freak was grinding into the bedspread,
nearly pushing into her warm entrance. He saw her
navel ring now, glinting in the rose-coloured light,
and he lightly grabbed the elastic band of her
panties. He began to pull them off but they caught

on something. He tugged gently and realized the rough elastic had grabbed one of her new lesions. Just enough to graze it and a tiny clear dot of fluid popped out. Nothing anyone would notice, but Nathan did. He was transfixed. The tiny dot caught the light just so, and he couldn't take his eyes off it. His hands started to tremble and his knees started shaking uncontrollably. It was just a dot, just a bit of fluid, but it was her disease. And here he was, her doctor, crouched over her like an animal, a primal beast with his own abnormality digging into the bed, his carnal desires overwhelming any scrap of dignity he may still possess within his soul. He felt like screaming, pounding his head against a wall, his beautiful Cynthia, what the fuck was he doing? What was he thinking? What kind of a freak was he? He couldn't do it. He felt sick, ill, disgusted, and crept back down the bed, pulling her skirt back down as he went. He closed her legs, mumbling apologies, berating himself, and then got off the bed to get dressed and carry her back out to the living room. Before he could pull his pants on, he felt the hairs on the back of his neck stand up and he froze. He thought he heard something. He looked over to the bed and Cynthia was sitting up, eyes wide open, staring at him.

Jesus, holy fucking Christ!

He stared at her, mouth open, face red, pants down. How much did she know? He debated running out of the room and never returning. But something about her look stopped him, confused him. She was cognitive, of that he was sure, but her eyes seemed accepting, not damning.

"Nathan," she said quietly. "Come here."

He couldn't. He just stared, but a tiny flicker of hope and disbelief lit up the darkness that had threatened to envelop his soul. She smiled then, a tender smile that miraculously connected both of them with its understanding. It touched something beneath their skin, it recognized things they were yet to discover. Nathan had never known such peace. He walked towards her slowly and she held out her scarred arms. He leaned over and she grasped the freak lightly with her cracked palm, pulling him onto her and, finally, into her. Nathan gave up everything to her then, and she took it all. Every inch.

They fell asleep facing each other, embraced. And while they slept, their demons at ease, all activity ceased. Way down deep, beneath the outer layers of Cynthia's epidermis, tiny microscopic skin cells were waking up to some bad news. Their party was over.

THE END.